Haunted Hikes of the A₁

Copyright © 20

Haunted Hikes of the Appalachian Hills and Hollers 2
Hiking Trails with legends, ghost stories, and abandoned places

ISBN: 978-1-940087-59-7
21 Crows Dusk to Dawn Publishing, 21 Crows, LLC

All rights reserved. No part of this book may be reproduced or transmitted in any form or by any means, electronic or mechanical, including photocopying, recording, or by any information storage and retrieval system, without permission in writing from the copyright owner. This is a work of fiction. Names, characters, places, and incidents either are the product of the author's imagination or are used fictitiously, and any resemblance to any actual persons, living or dead, events, or locales is entirely coincidental. This book was printed in the United States of America.

Always follow the rules/regulations in the areas you explore. Do not trespass. Do not enter areas after dark if it is not allowed—most parks are open dawn to dusk, but check times before entering. The information in this book like addresses are given to show where the story is located. Please check property ownership before visiting. QR codes and GPS guides were added to many trails so you can click on them with your phone camera and view the route. These routes may change or perform differently on different phones, so check for updates before relying on these solely.

People like to hear about ghost stories whether they believe in them or not. They like to tell them too.
My books are for all those people.

A Few Thoughts About Trails　　　　7

North Carolina

Pisgah National Forest　　　　16
Brown Mountain/Linville Gorge
Brown Mountain Lights

Pisgah National Forest　　　　25
Grandfather Mountain & Storyteller's Rock
Phantom Hiker

Roan High Bluff　　　　33
Cloudland Hotel
The Choir of the Dead of Roan Mountain

Roan Mountain　　　　39
Rhododendron Gardens
The Resounding Bell

Chimney Rock State Park　　　　43
Chimney Rock
The Extraordinary Phenomenon

Chimney Rock State Park and Hickory Nut Gorge　　　　47
The Little People of Hickory Nut Gorge

The Devil's Courthouse and Tennessee Bald　　　　51
The Devil's Courthouse

Great Smoky Mountains National Park　　　　57
Noland Creek Trail
Ghost Town

Virginia

Shenandoah National Park —Upper Pocosin Mission　　　　70
The Abandoned Old Pocosin Mission

Shenandoah National Park　　　　75
Potomac Appalachian Trail Club– Corbin Cabin
The Old Haunted Cabin in the Woods

George Washington & Jefferson National Forests　　　　87
Red Fox Trail to The Killing Rock (Forest Trail #205)
The Killing Rock Massacre

Combs Overlook —Raven Rock　　　　98
Bobbing Lantern Light (Jenkins, Ky but near Killing Rock)

Cumberland Gap National Historical Park—Gap Cave　　　　100
The Dead Soldier in Gap Cave

Kentucky

Pine Mountain State Resort Park   104
Clear Creek Hollow Trail
Ghost at Clear Creek Hollow

Pine Mountain State Resort Park   107
Chained Rock Trail
Chained Rock

Cathy Crockett Memorial Trail   110
Sloans Valley Tunnel
The Phantom Light of Sloans Valley Tunnel

Mammoth Cave National Park   112
Mammoth Cave
The Old Haunted Cave

Kentucky State Parks   118
Blue Licks Battlefield
They Rise from the Battlefield

Middle Creek National Battlefield   121
Unease

Maryland

Chesapeake & Ohio Canal National Historical Park   125
Monocacy Aqueduct
Old Raider's Treasure

Chesapeake & Ohio Canal National Historical Park   130
Paw Paw Tunnel
Headless Haunt

Green Ridge State Forest   134
Stickpile Tunnel
Stickpile

Chesapeake and Ohio Canal National Historical Park   139
Great Falls—Goldmine Trail
Goldmine Ghoul

Antietam National Battlefield—Burnside's Bridge   146
Phantoms of the Deadliest Battle

Chesapeake and Ohio Canal National Historical Park   150
Waste Weir between Locks 28 & 29
Ghost along the Waste Weir

Chesapeake and Ohio Canal National Historical Park   153
Haunted House Bend
Everlasting Swim

West Virginia

Dorsey's Knob Park and Disc Golf Course   160
The Red-headed Man of Dorsey's Knob

Twin Falls State Park   164
Hemlock Trail
Dead Cat Settles the Score

Twin Falls State Park   168
Falls Trail
The Headless Engineer of Cabin Creek

Twin Falls State Park   173
Poke Hollow Trail
That Thing up in Poke Holler

Twin Falls State Park   179
Bower Homestead
Old Haunted Homestead

Twin Falls State Park   180
Picnic Area and Woods Family Cemetery
Playground of the Dead

New River Gorge National Park   181
The Rend Trail
A Certain Likeness—Legend of McKinley Rock

Harpers Ferry   185
Appalachian Trail and Virginius Island Trail
A Haunted Hike through Harpers Ferry

Ohio

Ohio & Erie Canalway Nat'l Heritage Area—Lock 31   195
Lonesome Lock

Vinton County Parks—Moonville Tunnel   199
The Moonville Brakeman

Ohio State Parks/Watercraft—Lake Hope State Park   203
The Night Watchman

Conkle's Hollow State Nature Preserve—
Gorge Trail—Conkle's Hollow   207
After Dark

Wayne National Forest—Tinker's Cave   213
Ghostly Horses and the Dead Horse Thief

Ohio State Parks/Watercraft—Salt Fork State Park   217
Looking for Bigfoot

Pennsylvania

Abandoned Pennsylvania Turnpike—Southern Alleghenies Conservancy—Sideling Hill Tunnel — 224
Those Things That Lurk Within

Civilian Conservation Corps— Sideling Hill World War II German Prisoner of War Camp — 232
Ghostly Remnants of its Past

U.S. National Park Service-Gettysburg National Military Park—Spangler's Spring — 236
The Pale Blue Mist

U.S. National Park Service-Gettysburg National Military Park—Abraham Trostle & George Weikert Farms — 240
Haunted Battlefield Farms

U.S. National Park Service-Gettysburg National Military Park—Devil's Den — 244
Left Behind: Little Round Top and Devil's Den

Monterey Pass Battlefield Park & Museum Old Maria Furnace Road — 253
Hellhounds on his Heels

Citations — 262

A Little About the Trails in the Book—

A few things to know—

*I hiked all the areas in this book; some I returned because of seasonal closures. I learned a good lesson, and I will pass it on to you—***check for the most updated map of the hiking location online before visiting and call the controlling agency if you can***—there are many factors in the blink of an eye that can change the course of a trail system like fires or inclement weather. The maps I add in the book are for a general idea of the trails; each does not outline intricate details or daily updates. The types and quality of the hiking areas in this book vary widely from road beds to rugged paths to well-maintained nature trails. There are all types of hikers, so there are all types of trails including driving and wheelchair accessible.*

I use the terms below to describe each to give you a better idea of what you are getting into when you hit the trail. Always check ahead of time for trail closures due to seasonal weather-related hazards. I assume if you are searching out haunted hikes, I do not need to warn you about the risks associated with exploring for ghosts on or off the trail. Do not go on trails after dark in unsafe areas or trespass on private or public areas during off-hours.

Types of Trails:

Out-and-Back—Begin and end at the same location, returning along the same route. Typically day hike trails.

Loop—Begin and end at the same location, but follow a trail/trails that form a loop. Typically day hike trails.

Point-to-Point—Begin and end in different locations, usually for long-distance, extended trips for backpacking. Typically multiple-day hiking like the Appalachian Trail.

One-Way—Trails maintained in a loop and developed, for the safety of the natural area and hikers, so that hikers can only go one way from start to finish, unable to turn to go in the opposite direction. Often seen in cliff areas where it is unsafe to pass or areas with protected wildlife species/plants to maintain minimal human interference.

Spur—Trail that branches off a main trail and leads to a dead end, usually at a point of interest such as an overlook or historical feature.

Quality of Trails:

Developed Trails—Man-made paths wide enough to comfortably hike with grass and brush typically removed. Features are usually added, such as steps, ramps, and bridges. They require routine maintenance.

Multi-use Trail—Used by pedestrians but may also be used by bikers and horseback riders.

Backcountry Trail—Not maintained and usually have no features like restrooms or camping facilities. Experienced hikers use them.

Nature Trail—Routinely maintained and usually offer interpretive signs along the path.

Trail Road—Unpaved lane or road that vehicles may use.

Rail-trail—A paved or graveled trail made from an abandoned railroad corridor/tracks.

Elements to Heed When Hiking Abandoned/Remote Places:

I added QR codes to many trails so you can click on them with your phone camera and view the route. These routes may change or perform differently on different phones, so check for updates before relying solely on these. The time the mapping system stated it would take me to get from one point to the next was rarely the same amount of time it took me to hike the trail—it took me longer.

- When old buildings are abandoned, old outhouse pits and wells are sometimes not covered, and the brush grows around them. Watch where you step!
- Mark your starting location on your positioning and mapping devices before your hike so you can retrace your steps if you get lost.
- Leave an itinerary of your travel destinations with someone before you depart.
- Bear, elk, and large predators share the same paths as humans. I have seen many on or near the trails in this book. I kept my distance and gave them the right of way. Be aware of your surroundings so you do not stumble into their path and startle them. But also be conscious of the fact that they may sense you long before you realize they are there. Always carry a light source so that if your journey lasts into the dark, you can light the path and not stumble upon a wild animal.

Map Notations:

⟹ Hiking trail route.
⟹ Hiking Trail Note or Location.

When using QR codes or any mapping method, make sure you re-check the mapping system before hiking for accuracy and changes to the trail.

A Little Bit about GPS Coordinates and QR Codes Used in the Book—

Using GPS tracking and a very basic way to use tracking on your desktop or phone:

Roads, trails, and haunted locations are often remote and do not have a street number or name. I use GPS because the two numbers given, called coordinates, uniquely identify a precise location. Hikers can enter coordinates by typing or copying and pasting them into the search box of a mapping app and clicking the Search button (magnifying glass). The location will display with a red pin on the map and details (if available) on the left. If directions are needed, an origin can be added with a simple click of the "directions" button, which will pull up a box so a starting point can be typed.

Here are the coordinates for the haunted town of Moonville: 39.308828, -82.324810

A minus sign before the second number indicates that the location is *west* of the prime meridian. If a minus sign is located in front of the first number, it will show degrees *south* of the equator.

If that flew right over your head, no big deal. Just understand that it is important that the *minus sign* is with the correct number because the placement of the minus sign is crucial. Do not confuse the two and accidentally get them backward because this coordinate -39.308828, 82.324810 (noting the minus sign is in the first number this time) will take you to the center of the Indian Ocean and 250 miles from the closest land!

I use QR Codes as an easy way to share the hiking trail I followed to a specific site with readers who can pull the route up on their phone and get an idea of the course. I will add that QR Codes, mapping systems, and courses are not perfect. Trails change and may close due to rockfalls, other obstructions, or updates. A hiker's mapping system may be set up for a shorter route or only roadways, taking them on a different path or even on property that is now private or closed to the public. Areas change, and sometimes, a newer, better trail is available. Always route your origin and destination before leaving for a trip, check for trail closures and revisions, and ensure the route is safe.

How to use QR Codes:

Hold your smartphone camera app to the QR code as if taking a picture and allow it to focus in the viewfinder. The phone will recognize the code as you move it toward the QR code (you may have to move it back and forth slowly a few times to get the camera to focus). When you see your mapping app name show up, touch it, and the map will show up in your mapping system.

A Note about using QR codes for the trails in this book:

Sometimes, when I set up hiking paths on apps, the mapping system does not recognize a designated trail. Instead, it will automatically find the closest roadway and take users along this route. Most commonly, this occurs when there is a new bridge, structure, or path that mappers have not added to the program.

To correct the irregularity, I have to set up extra stops along the hiking route to override the programs that desire to take hikers in another direction. That said, if your mapping app states you have arrived at a location along the route and there appears to be nothing there, it is only one of the stops I added to solve the conflict with the mapping system. You just need to continue onward.

Always pull up the QR code and map before you leave for your hike. Check to make sure that it takes you along the correct route. You may also find other interesting trails nearby that you wish to hike or places you want to see that I have not written about in this book. And do not rely on the app's hiking systems so much that you follow it off a cliff. It does not have a conscience or a sense of right or wrong. And it certainly does not have an IQ, so no matter how many apps you have on the phone, you are still smarter than it. So do not rely solely on your phone and the maps. Use your judgment first.

North Carolina

Pisgah National Forest Brown Mountain & Linville Gorge
Burke County, North Carolina
Caldwell County, North Carolina

Brown Mountain Lights

Mysterious lights have appeared around Brown Mountain for centuries. For those who dare journey to see them, there is a trail—

Within the enormous Appalachian Mountain range that spans seven states lies the smaller Blue Ridge. It is still grand, extending eight states across Virginia, the western edge of North Carolina, part of South Carolina, and even a corner of Georgia. Yet, those who pause to take in her grandeur from a roadway overlook cannot help but feel small; the range seems never-ending. These mystical mountains are among the oldest in the world, and the plants and trees, to protect themselves from heat, emit a gas (hydrocarbon called isoprene), which reacts with the atmosphere and creates a bluish haze—hence, the name: Blue Ridge.

Brown Mountain lies within this range, and something strange happens here. Mysterious lights float on Brown Mountain in the Pisgah National Forest near Morganton, North Carolina. Some have witnessed red lights, and others white with a halo, pale yellow like a frosted globe, orange, or blue. Some glow as small as candlelight, while others are the size of a firework rocket. People have witnessed them flow along the forest floor and climb high toward the sky for centuries. However, their popularity gained significant leverage between 1909 and 1921 when local newspapers began publishing articles about the mysterious lights.

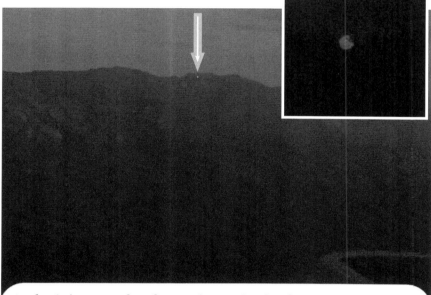

Author's images taken from Wiseman's View between 9:00 p.m. and midnight on a cool, damp evening in October—I could see the lights with my naked eye. Catching them on my cell phone or GoPro camera was more difficult. Neither were night vision cameras, which I highly recommend using. However, I did notice one vivid blue ball deep in the valley that stayed still, then weaved away. I also viewed many large white, fuzzy balls along the mountain range that moved erratically up and down, brightening and fading over the lapse of seconds to a minute. At first, I thought these were nothing more than car headlights appearing and disappearing through gaps in trees on an up-and-down mountain roadway until I realized the location of the strange lights was along a sheer cliff wall.

Although scientists and the curious, including the Smithsonian, U.S. Weather Service, and U.S. Geological Survey, have extensively studied these lights, their origin remains unknown. Those who have explored their peculiar appearance have yet to provide a solid explanation. Local legends explain that the activity began in the year 1200 after a great battle between Catawba and Cherokee, fighting over the territory of Brown Mountain. After one bloody fight, women came out with pine-lit torches, searching in vain for the warriors who never returned. The lights are the torches of these long-dead phantoms. Another local story recalls a pregnant wife who lived on the mountain and who was slain by her husband. Twinkling lights led neighbors to her corpse, and they discovered the murder. Townspeople hanged the offender for his crime. The lights still shine to remind other wrongdoers that they too will be caught and brought to justice should they commit some dastardly deed.

Some have suggested the lights may be phosphorescent (glowing) light emitted by fungi, Will-o'-the-wisp or swamp gas, or gases from a rich cache of minerals, and even aliens. In October 1913, D. B. Sterrett, of the U.S. Geological Team, spent a few days investigating the mysterious lights and concluded that the phenomena were nothing more than the bright headlamps on westbound Southern Railway locomotives working their way through the mountains.

A type of bioluminescent fungi— Some have suggested the lights come from bioluminescent fungi growing on old stumps and trees like beech and oak. They use molecules called luciferins that, when mixed with enzymes and oxygen, react and release light. It is the same compound found in the abdomens of lightning bugs that make them glow.

However, after a severe flood in 1916 obliterated the train tracks and bridges, residents still witnessed the lights, and Sterrett's theory was rejected by many.

A minister spent a month's vacation in the mountains and claimed to see the light 12 to 15 times in 1914. He described it as appearing like the Roman candles and fireworks commonly set off at Christmas during this time period, sometimes zigzagging toward the sky. In 1916, an expedition was organized by a local doctor, with teams of men set up at separate areas, including Adams Knob and Brown Mountain. The men took turns as lookouts, and the doctor advised these lookouts, who were supplied with pistols, that they were to shoot three times upon seeing any lights. There were four appearances of the lights—three on Brown Mountain and one on Adams Knob. Incredibly, when the light occurred, it was only visible to the team upon which mountain they were studying. Although the expedition did not determine an answer for the source, they discovered it was not a light emanating from a cabin, a train headlamp, or a moonshine distillery secreted far from watchful eyes. Even nowadays, the lights can be seen sporadically on the mountain, usually after rain in the fall.

There are two main viewing areas:
1) Wiseman's View—Hike to an Observation Deck
2) Brown Mountain Overlook—View by Roadside

1) Wiseman's View:

This viewing area is named for Lafayette "Fate" Wiseman, an early cattle drover, who camped here while grazing his cattle. As a child of about 12 and around 1854, he witnessed the lights while camping with his father. It is the oldest report of the mysterious lights. Later, his great nephew and country music star Scotty Wiseman wrote the song The *Legend of the Brown Mountain Lights* around 1961 after hearing the legend passed down in his family. As it was told to him, the light was the lantern carried by a ghostly slave still searching for his southern planter owner who lost his way while hunting and never returned home. The song made Brown Mountain a popular place to visit and search for the spirited lights.

The trail is paved at Wiseman's View—the upper viewing area shown offers wheelchair hikers access to watch for the lights, although a fairly steep slope might require assistance. Just a few steps below are the stone viewing areas.

Waiting at an overlook for darkness to come—On this night, I saw the mysterious Brown Mountain Lights and a huge meteor brightening the sky. There was also a creepy line of lights that looked like a train moving across the black sky, which I was sure was either Santa Claus and his sleigh or aliens. I later learned it was a SpaceX Starlink sent by a privately owned spaceflight and satellite communications company.

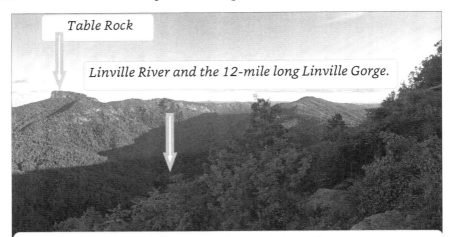

Table Rock

Linville River and the 12-mile long Linville Gorge.

Another view is from Wiseman's Overlook from the stone observation area perched above a cliff to the right. The Linville River is about 1500 feet below, central to this image.

An interesting story of Linville Falls and the gorge and how it acquired its name:

In the autumn of 1766, John Linville (about 28 years old) and John Williams (about 19 years old) headed from their settlement in the Yadkin River Valley into the Blue Ridge Mountains along with several packhorses for a hunt about 10 miles below the location of Linville Falls today. Along with them was John's father, 55-year-old William, whose health was declining, but believed an excursion with his son might help boost his condition.

As the sun began to rise one morning during their journey, William Linville awakened with a start and quickly roused the two younger men. He told them he had a vivid dream that Native Americans had broken into their camp and massacred the men. Being of poor health, William implored his son and the other young man to flee as soon as possible without him, as the older man felt he could not keep up during a chase. As William tried desperately to convince them of the danger, a party of what was thought to be Shawnee or Cherokee who had been concealing themselves in the brush let out a barrage of gunshot. Both William Linville and his son died. A bullet hit John Williams in the leg, but he escaped on a packhorse where, four days later, he made it to the safety of a settlement. Daniel Boone, a friend of the Linville family, returned to the gorge, found the mutilated bodies, and buried them.

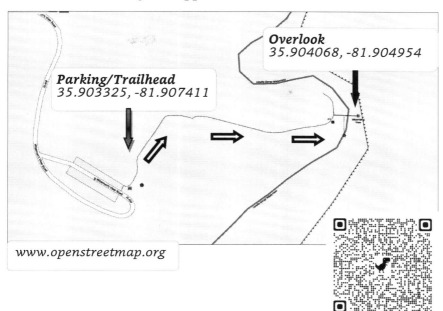

Wiseman's View
Parking/Trailhead:
Scenic Overlook Parking Lot
Old North Carolina 105 to Wiseman's View Road
Marion, North Carolina 28752
(35.903325, -81.907411)
The drive to this viewing spot is not recommended for low-lying vehicles. The 4.9-mile (one-way) road is gravel with many deep potholes, ruts, and parts of the road are subject to washouts. There is a single vault restroom (no lighting, so bring a flashlight). No water is available.

Hike: 0.2 miles, one-way. Easy. Out and back.
The short trail to two observation decks is tree-lined and paved. A third upper-level deck is great for those in wheelchairs (there is a less-sloped bypass on the route for the steeper walking descent). There is plenty of room to view from the decks and the stony ledge. If you plan on staying a while, you may wish to bring a blanket or foldup chair to sit on for comfort.
Observation decks: (35.904068, -81.904954)

2) Brown Mountain View Overlook:

Parking/Trailhead:
Newland, North Carolina 28657
(35.942552, -81.842010)
The easy route—you can stop at a roadside overlook location to observe the lights, pulling right off Jonas Ridge/Highway 181 in Newland, and it is just a few steps to see the mountain and, perhaps, watch the lights. The pull-off has picnic tables, a parking area, and historical/informational signage showing a visual map denoting the mountain range, including where the peak of Brown Mountain is located, about 2.4 miles from the overlook.

Brown Mountain View Overlook

Pisgah National Forest Grandfather Mountain & Storyteller's Rock
Avery County, North Carolina
Caldwell County, North Carolina
Watauga County, North Carolina

Phantom Hiker

Auto road along Grandfather Mountain, Linville, N.C. —1912

In earlier years, Grandfather Mountain, named for the face of an old man seen on its cliffs, was a privately owned tourist attraction and a nature preserve with a rough road and trail leading to an incredible craggy view. In the early 1950s, one of the successors of the property, Hugh Morton, built a mile-high swinging bridge.

Grandfather Mountain was named by early settlers who saw the face of an old man in the cliffs. Image: National Park Service

After the death of Mister Morton and around 2009, his heirs transferred the ownership of 1/3 of the land, including the bridge and surrounding landmarks, to the Grandfather Mountain Stewardship Foundation. This non-profit group opens the attraction, including the Mile-High Swinging Bridge, the Nature Museum, and Wildlife Habitat, for an admission fee that goes back to preserving the mountain.

The remaining 2/3 of the backcountry area of the mountain was sold as a state park. This area has no fees for hiking, although hikers must fill out a permit for free when taking the trails so that if they do not return to their car on time, rangers will know where to search for them. The landscape is rugged, wild, and extreme. Weather can be severe and change quickly on the mountain—squalls and record-high wind speeds are possible. Yet, this deeply forested area and the 12 miles of trails within are where a ghostly visitor appears.

The cause of the hiker's appearance has never been explained, but for hundreds and hundreds of years people have been hunting and logging and exploring its expanse. Some say that a man got lost on the mountain long ago during a storm. He perished, and his body was never found.

The backcountry Tanawha/Nuwati Trail to Storyteller's Rock on the park's East Side is the perfect place to start searching for the ghostly hiker at Grandfather Mountain.

He has a weathered face, beard and wears outdated clothes. Sometimes he is seen with a walking stick. Upon his back, there is an old-fashioned rucksack, a primitive, simple backpack. The backcountry trails can be steep, craggy, and rocky, with stream crossings and strenuous climbs. There are fewer hikers passing one another along these routes. That said, when someone does cross paths, most people take notice, gesturing with a friendly nod or greeting with a "hello" or "How's it going?" Some people have witnessed the ghost and even stated that the mysterious man on the trail approached within arm's distance. However, the phantom hiker does not acknowledge those he meets, never answers, and disappears not long after.

Tlanuwa (Tanawha) means Black Eagle—the giant bird of Cherokee legend that sometimes snatched up a child when flying above Cherokee settlements. A medicine man climbed to their nest to stop them and threw four young birds into a river. A great snake, Uktena, rose and ate the baby birds. Enraged, the Tlanuwa caught the snake and flew into the sky, and neither Tlanuwa nor Uktena were seen again.

Four Trails of Grandfather Mountain:

Grandfather Mountain offers 11 trails ranging from short, easy walks to long, difficult treks along rugged rock trails and across craggy peaks. The backcountry trail to Storyteller's Rock offers one area where those who have taken the route have witnessed the ghostly hiker. This trail can also provide a starting point, with proper preparations, for longer trips. If choosing lengthier journeys, hikers need to check maps, weather updates, and the Grandfather Mountain State Park website, as many of the trails are long and strenuous. Park hours vary—cars cannot be left in some lots overnight and hiking cliff areas at night is dangerous. Other hiking routes at the park are strenuous and rough-going with cables and ladders.

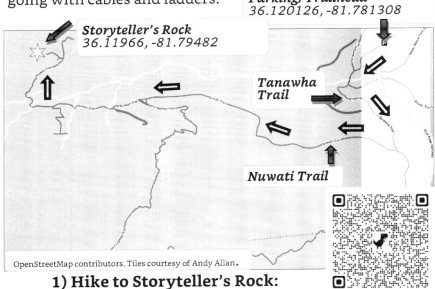

Parking/Trailhead 36.120126, -81.781308
Storyteller's Rock 36.11966, -81.79482
Tanawha Trail
Nuwati Trail

OpenStreetMap contributors. Tiles courtesy of Andy Allan.

1) Hike to Storyteller's Rock:

Parking: Boone Fork Parking Area
Blue Ridge Parkway, Laurel Springs, North Carolina 28644 (36.120126, -81.781308)

Hike a backcountry trail: Tanawha Trail to Nuwati Trail to Storyteller's Rock and Boone Bowl View. It is an easy trail along an old logging route, but with lots of rocks and roots, and hikers must cross small streams.

Trailhead: (36.119892, -81.781576) Start at the far end of Boone Fork Parking Area. A sign at the end of the small lot marks the Tanawha Trail, which leads to the Nuwati Trail.

There is a kiosk at the Nuwati Trail Trailhead. Hikers must register there. Make sure that you have your vehicle license number for the form and note the park's open and closing hours.

Hike: 1.4 miles, one-way. Out and back.
Storyteller's Rock: (36.11966, -81.79482)
Take the Tanawha Trail 0.4 miles to the Nuwati Trail (Blue Blaze). Turn right on the Nuwati Trail. Follow the trail for about 1.0 miles. There are three Back Country Primitive Campsites along this trail – The Hermitage, Storyteller's Rock, and The Refuge. Hikers will pass The Hermitage. At the second, Storyteller's Rock Campsite, you will see a wooden sign with VIEW revealing that the trail for Storyteller's Rock begins to the left. Hikers must scramble up tall boulders to Storyteller's Rock. The climb to the observation point is rugged, steep, and unsuitable for children.

View from Storyteller's Rock—

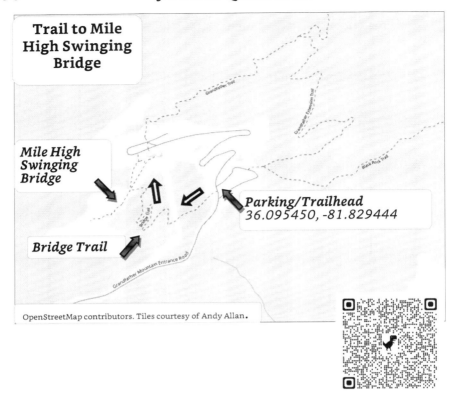

2) Hike the Mile High Swinging Bridge:

Parking/Trailhead: Grandfather Mountain Lower Parking
Off Grandfather Mountain Entrance Road
Linville, North Carolina 28646
(36.095450, -81.829444)

Hike to Mile High Swinging Bridge: 0.4 miles, one-way. Out and back. One of the more popular but crowded hikes is the trail to Mile High Swinging Bridge.
When entering Grandfather Mountain State Park from the Swinging Bridge area, hikers can park in the Lower Parking Area and take the steps, then a winding, forested path to the Mile High Swinging Bridge and after to Linville Peak. There is a fee; purchasing tickets online before the trip is best.

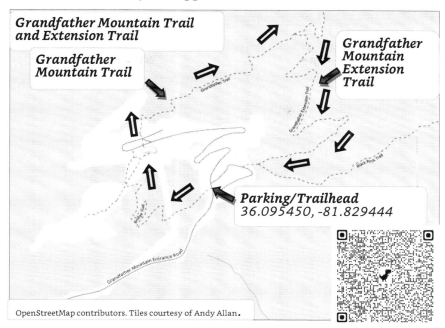

3) Hike the Grandfather Mountain Trail *Plus* Grandfather Mountain Extension Trail:

Parking/Trailhead: Grandfather Mountain Lower Parking Off Grandfather Mountain Entrance Road
Linville, North Carolina 28646
(36.095450, -81.829444)

Hike: Grandfather Mountain Trail—(Blue Blazed) and Extension Trail: 1.4 miles. Loop. For a longer and more strenuous trek, hikers can continue another 1.0 miles along the Grandfather Mountain Trail from the Mile High Swinging Bridge /Upper Parking Area and back to the Lower Parking Area via the Grandfather Mountain Trail and the Grandfather Extension Trail (Red Blazed). Cross the parking lot by the entrance road and take the steps to the Grandfather Mountain Trail. At about 0.4 miles, take a right onto the Grandfather Trail Extension for about 0.6 miles to the Lower Parking Area.

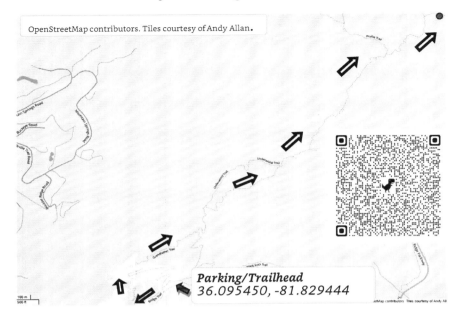

Parking/Trailhead
36.095450, -81.829444

4) Hike Grandfather Mountain Trail To Calloway Peak:

Parking/Trailhead: Grandfather Mountain Lower Parking Off Grandfather Mountain Entrance Road Linville, North Carolina 28646 (36.095450, -81.829444)

Hike to Calloway Peak: 2.0–2.7 miles, one-way. Out and Back. Strenuous: Grandfather Trail (Blue Blazed). Start at the lower parking area as if taking the bridge trail and then through the parking area to Grandfather Mountain Trail. Hand-over-hand, with cables and ladders. Not for those afraid of heights. Alpine trail that crosses the entire summit ridge from the trailhead at Swinging Bridge to Calloway Peak. Strenuous. Features areas with cables and ladders.

Fun Fact: In the Academy Award Winning film Forrest Gump, Gump rises from his porch at his Greenbow, Alabama home and decides to go for a little run for "no particular reason." It turns into a 3-year, 2-month, 14-day, and 16-hour journey across the U.S. At one point, he and his followers are shown running up a curve in a roadway. This scene was filmed at none other than Grandfather Mountain State Park with the Blue Ridge Mountains in the background. You can drive up this switchback; there is a sign with "Forrest Gump Curve." You cannot hike it, but like many who honk their horns as they barrel through the Blue Ridge Parkway's tunnels, some shout, "Run, Forrest, Run!" as they pass by this spot.

Forrest Gump Curve Grandfather Mountain Entrance Road Linville, North Carolina 28646 (36.092438, -81.836033)

Roan High Bluff—Cloudland Hotel
Mitchell County, North Carolina
Carter County, Tennessee

The Choir of the Dead—Roan Mountain

Cloudland Hotel and patron, 1905— Image: Library of Congress

Roan Mountain, a high ridge of five summits in the Appalachian Mountains, encompasses much of the Roan Highlands and straddles the Tennessee and North Carolina borders. Two of its peaks, Roan High Bluff and Roan High Knob, are divided from Round Bald, Jane Bald, and Grassy Ridge Bald by Carver's Gap. The latter, known as grassy balds, get their names from their covering of thick grasses and scrubby shrubs instead of forest growth.

Local folklore tells that Daniel Boone would ride his favorite horse that had the unique roan pattern (a blend of white and colored hair within its coat) through this mountain. On one trip, the horse became lame, and Boone left it atop the summit to heal. When he returned sometime later, the horse was well again and plump from feeding on the thick grasses. Those who saw the horse when it made its home there for this short period began to call the highland *Roan Mountain* for the horse's roan pattern. Others say that Roan Mountain received its name for the crimson shade of the rhododendron flowers that grow abundantly on the peaks. At one time, though, legends were told that the petals of the rhododendron were pure white. However, the Native Americans in the area fought often, and so much blood was spilled on the land the flowers turned crimson forever after.

It is along this mountain and near the summit of Roan High Knob that Union General John T. Wilder built an enormous three-story, 166-room lodge and called it Cloudland Hotel for the hazy clouds that cloaked the mountain and lodge most of the time. In the late 1800s and early 1900s, wealthy guests could rent a carpeted, well-appointed room at the hotel for $2.50 a night. The fee included three delicious meals and recreational activities such as ballroom dancing in a great room on a solid maple floor with musicians playing piano and violin. Or those who were not teetotalers could unwind with a drink in the dining area. *Half of the dining area*, that is, because visitors passed along rumors that there was a white chalk line down the center of the restaurant, showing the division between North Carolina and Tennessee. You could only imbibe alcohol on the Tennessee side, where it was legally served, but certainly not on the North Carolina side, where the laws prohibited it. It seems the local Mitchell County, North Carolina sheriff would hide in the shadows waiting for folks to break the law so he could cart them off to jail.

Hiking the misty trail is like walking into an enchanted forest—

That aside, and most importantly for the guests, the hotel offered them the ability to relax, and many did just that on the hotel's porches, which overlooked the beautiful mountain range. There, the clientele could watch the sunset or feel like they were being pulled into a magical world as layers of fog surrounded them in a thick blanket of fairy-like, enchanting mist. Yet it was on the days when the mighty winds snatched up the thick clouds on the mountain that something unearthly fell on visitors' ears just outside the doors. Those who heard it were sure it was not the wail of harsh winds after a storm whipped through the trees and shrubs. Instead, it was the ethereal echo of voices ebbing and flowing with the air as if a multitude of angels were singing, a great choir practicing for Judgement Day. Or old lost souls still trying to find their way home off the mountain.

Perhaps the chanting was not so God-sent; some believed the devil's minions were to blame for the source, and those sounds were spewed up from the bowels of Hell—the fiendish cries and screams of demons lamenting their eternal fate and desiring to lure the curious to the same doom. And possibly, sometimes, they did. One young man staying at the hotel explored one day to locate the music's source, but a thunderstorm waylaid his hike. He sought refuge in a cave from the howls and moans that whipped up from the hillsides and accompanied the sudden onslaught of wind and rain. Inside the cave, he tumbled, hit his head, and knocked himself out. While unconscious, he had a horrible nightmare of a choir of demons and phantoms singing to him in all sorts of torment.

There is a remnant of an old building just before the short climb to the ruins of the Cloudland Hotel. The Appalachian Trail is marked with white blazes, as seen on the tree above.

The Cloudland Hotel lay abandoned in 1910. It took little time for the structure to fall into ruins as it stood upon the mountaintop blasted by hard winds and inclement weather.

The place where the hotel once stood in its grandeur. Only a small overlook at the far end remains—and the clouds and ghostly songs as they whip past in the wind. Even on this day, layers of heavy mist surrounded me, and rode with the breeze through the valleys.

Many believe nothing remains of its celebrated past but a bare spot on the old grounds. Not so; hikers taking the Appalachian Trail past the place where Cloudland Hotel once stood near Toll House Gap have witnessed the same ghostly singing heard by guests at the lodge more than 140 years ago. The chorus of the dead works its way from some mysterious location that nobody can pinpoint, surrounds those stopping for a moment to appraise the crooning tune, then envelopes those who hear its song in its shadowy embrace.

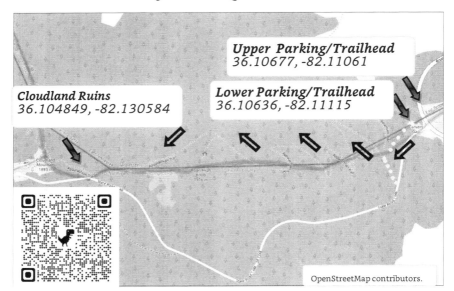

Hike the Appalachian Trail on Roan Mountain to the remnants of the old Cloudland Hotel and perhaps witness the Choir of the Dead.

Hike: 1.9 miles, one-way. Out and back. Rugged with stones. Moderate.

Parking/Trailhead: Two Parking Areas:
1) Carvers Gap *Upper* Parking:
TN-143, Roan Mountain, TN 37687 (36.10677, -82.11061)
If parking in the upper lot, look for the Appalachian Trail at the end of the lot by the guardrail (36.10677, -82.11061). You can see where it connects from across the road. Or you can walk around the road bend to the lower parking level. The Lower Parking Trailhead leading to the Appalachian Trail is beside the restrooms at the far end of the lower parking lot. Hike the trail and turn right, where the white blazes begin at the main trail. Turning left, will take you to the roadway and an alternate route back to the parking area along the street.

2) Carvers Gap *Lower* Parking Area
TN-143, Roan Mountain, TN 37687 (36.10636, -82.11115)
Trailhead: (36.106518, -82.111260) The Lower Parking Trailhead leading to the Appalachian Trail is beside the restrooms at the far end of the lower parking lot. Hike the trail and turn right, where the white blazes begin at the main trail.

Roan Mountain— Rhododendron Gardens
Mitchell County, North Carolina

The Resounding Bell

Rhododendron Gardens at Roan Mountain—

In days long in the past when livestock had grazed the fields in the valley below Roan Mountain to little more than nubby stubs, farmers herded their cattle up slopes to feed on the lush spring and summer grasses growing there. As there were many farmers, each would mark their livestock with notches to identify their ownership.

Everyone shared the mountain meadows' bounty of food—except one cattle owner. This wealthy landowner stood out among the others, always having the largest herd of cows. He was constantly pushing his cattle earlier, farther, and faster up the summit than the others so his livestock would get the highest quality vegetation and the largest field. He also owned the biggest bull that anyone had seen in these parts. This bull donned a large bell held on by a strap on its neck so the herder could keep track of him. It was exceptionally raucous and was said to ring so loudly that even in a thunderstorm, those taking the mountain paths could hear its clanging one mile away. This bell was known to resound so loudly that it spooked the other cattle at times into a stampede, endangering the newborn calves around it. Huge and hulking, the monstrous beast would lead his large herd of chubby cows up the incline each year with bell clattering and rattling, most times forcing his way through the smaller herds. Should another bull challenge him, he whipped his head about, snorted, then attacked the other poor creature until it was nearly dead.

The lush grasses of Roan Mountain were the perfect grazing pastures for local livestock—

Townspeople often grumbled that the rich landowner's herd left little for the others. At some point, and with so many cows feasting on the grasses, he would overgraze the Roan. The others' cattle would starve. The farmer's greedy behavior continued for years. Then one spring, he bragged that this was the year he was bringing up the biggest herd anyone would ever see, and he did. The community watched in awe and resentment as the monster of a bull strolled up the mountain in front of his cows, bullying its way past the other herds with its bell rattling and banging with every wag of his thick neck. On he went, higher and higher and finally to where the lushest grasses were blowing in the wind, and fog followed thickly above. The bull paused there and sniffed the breeze while the mist wisped around its wide body as if it, like the other bulls, was too frightened to come close. Then, a shot rang out from deep in the fog and from someone hidden in the balsams. The massive bull keeled forward and dropped dead, its bell rattling boisterously. The mist closed in, and whoever had fired the shot slipped away without notice.

Dead, the bull may be. But it never left Roan Mountain. On foggy days when the clouds seem to dodge the sky and sweep low over the rhododendrons and grasses on the mountain where the Cloudland Hotel once stood and all the way to where the Rhododendron Gardens are today, some have heard the loud clang and rattle of its bell while he leads a ghostly herd of cows to the richest grasses.

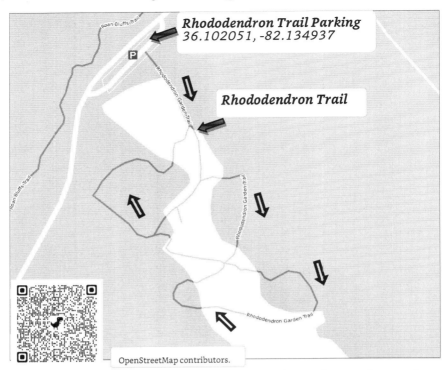

Hike the Rhododendron Trail and, perhaps, hear the ghostly bell of the bull.

Parking/Trailhead:
Rhododendron Gardens (The peak bloom time is usually mid-June, give or take a week, due to different weather conditions.)
147 Garden Road (Off State Road 1348)
Bakersville, North Carolina 28705
There is a fee to hike the gardens.
(36.102051, -82.134937)

Hike: About 0.5 to 1.0 miles. Loop. The trail (where witnesses have heard the legendary cowbell) features an Upper (wheelchair accessible) and Lower loop (has several steps). The trail passes through Catawba rhododendrons. There are 16 interpretive stops on the upper loop trail.

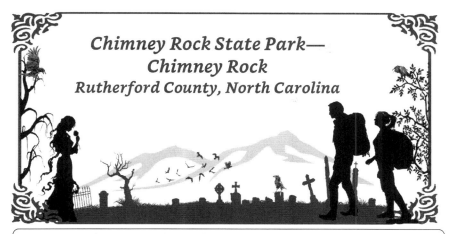

Chimney Rock State Park—Chimney Rock
Rutherford County, North Carolina

The Extraordinary Phenomenon

The top of Chimney Rock—where mysterious visions are witnessed.

Chimney Rock, on the edge of the Blue Ridge Mountains, is a 315-foot-high naturally formed granite outcropping 2,280 feet above sea level that can be seen from miles away. It has been sitting there for well over 535 million years, so it would not seem surprising that sometime during its long existence, something mysterious would happen in its midst.

And it did. Around six in the evening of July of 1806, eight-year-old Elizabeth Reaves called out to her 11-year-old brother Morgan while she stood a little apart from him in the family's cornfield. She declared that a man was standing on Chimney Rock, about ¾ mile away. Of course, Morgan did not believe her, and from his vantage point, he could not see the granite outcropping. No one had ever seen anyone scale the huge standing stone; it was nearly straight up. However, his little sister was insistent, stating that it appeared the man was rolling rocks or picking up sticks. So Morgan went to where she was standing and looked up, shocked. He saw not just one man but thousands of people flying in the air. He hollered out in astonishment at this mysterious sight. It was not long before the children's mother, Patsy Reaves, heard the child's call. She and a daughter joined in to behold the extraordinary wonder.

The group gazed at the strange phenomenon for nearly an hour, watching the people flit through the air. They could not discern any gender, just that there were small figures and large figures. Finally, Patsy Reaves had the foresight to call upon a local man named Robert Siercy as another set of eyes to behold this marvel appearing at the outcropping. Of course, he thought it was foolishness, but after Missus Reaves sent a second message, he reluctantly made his way there. At first, and once there, Siercy saw nothing. Then while he gazed toward where the others watched, he caught glittery white human-like forms wearing white garments moving in a semi-circle near the rock. Eventually, a few glided higher, then appeared to coax the rest upwards into the heavens before all faded from sight.

Strangely, when the group with Missus Reaves watched the events, a man a few miles away witnessed an unusual, bright rainbow, although there were no clouds or rain.

Then, only a few years later, in 1811, others saw a ghostly battle atop the rock. Winged horses circled the sky, and men armed with swords fought while those within view could hear swords clacking and the moans of the wounded. For ten minutes, the battle raged, then one army appeared defeated, and the other disappeared into the dark.

Visitors wishing to get to the top of Chimney Rock can take an elevator and a short series of steps. Or they can walk a longer series of 499 steps, one-way, from the bottom. Both allow hikers to stand where the extraordinary phenomenon occurred.

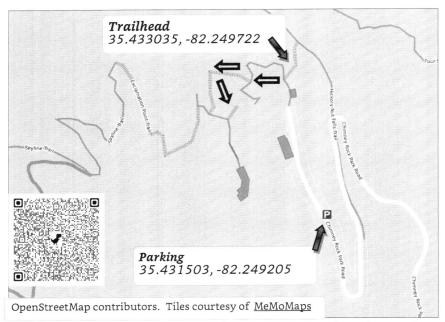

OpenStreetMap contributors. Tiles courtesy of MeMoMaps

Hike the steps to the top of Chimney Rock, where the mysterious events were witnessed—
Parking/Trailhead: Chimney Rock State Park—Chimney Park Road Chimney Rock, North Carolina 28720 There is a fee to enter this park. (35.431503, -82.249205)

1) Hike: Outcropping Trail—up to 0.5 miles, one-way. Stairway to Chimney Rock (499 wooden steps)—the trail has a combination of steps and switchbacks leading to popular points of interest like the Opera Box, Devil's Head, and Exclamation Point before making it to Chimney Rock. **Trailhead:** (35.433035, -82.249722)

2) Hike: Exclamation Point Trail —0.2 miles, one-way. (leads to 200 feet above Chimney Rock). 330 steps, one-way.

Elevator Access: Wheelchair/Hiking (or for those not wishing to hike the many steps) There is an elevator tunnel near the parking lot. A half-minute elevator ride takes visitors from the parking lot level to the upper gift shop. There is a view along a bridge of 75 miles, including Lake Lure and the Blue Ridge Foothills. Chimney Rock is within a short distance, although visitors must take 40 steps to get to the very top. If visitors must take the elevator, please check with the park beforehand to ensure it is not receiving normal maintenance on the day of entry!

Chimney Rock State Park And Hickory Nut Gorge
Rutherford County, North Carolina

The Little People of Hickory Nut Gorge

Atop Chimney Rock and looking out over Hickory Nut Gorge—a place of Cherokee legends.

At one time, a community of Yunwi Tsundsdi, little forest spirits or fairies, lived within the caves on the mountainsides in the Hickory Nut Gorge, a 14-mile canyon filled with waterfalls and granite cliffs, the mouth of which is located at Chimney Rock State Park.

Most of the time, Yunwi Tsundsdi remain invisible and loathe being bothered by outsiders. They savor more than a bit of merriment amongst themselves and spend half of their day dancing and drumming music. Yet if they show themselves, these magical little people appear with hair so long it nearly reaches the earth, are knee-high, and are attractive and perfectly proportioned like a human child. Usually caring and kind, they will help humans in need and reward them graciously if humans help them. When people get lost in the forest, they will show them the way home, especially little children they gently guide back to their parents. They also tend to sick humans if they find them.

That said, it is highly advised never to disrespect or hurt a Yunwi Tsundsdi as they dole out punishment severely. Should a human accidentally stumble across their communities or dwellings, they will cast a spell that will make the human forget. Some intruders are so affected by this particularly potent spell that they become befuddled, and it spoils their ability to find their way home. After this bewitchment, hapless victims wander in a stupor and aimlessly for years, many dying from starvation. If someone saw the little people and lived through the enchantment, they could not speak of it for seven years.

One day while hunting, a warrior found tiny children's footprints in the snow and followed them to a cave. It belonged to Yunwi Tsundsdi; they welcomed him with open arms, fed him, and then let him go. But they warned the hunter should he tell where he had been and mention that he had seen them, the man would die. So he made his way home, and the others at his camp were curious why it took him so long to return. They questioned the hunter day after day, and anxious to tell them regardless of the warning, the man broke his silence and told his friends of the Yunwi Tsundsdi. The next day, they found the man dead.

The Cherokee shared some of the outlying areas with the Yunwi Tsundsdi. The Hickory Nut Gorge was the most direct path through the valley where they needed to travel to trade for the tobacco they used as medicinals and in spiritual rituals to carry prayers to Great Spirit Unetlanvhi, the Creator. However, the wary Yunwi Tsundsdi guarded the area ferociously. The Cherokee devised many plans and attempted to pass through the gorge, but those men brave enough to journey there never returned. One young man wishing to show his prowess to his elders snuck off during the night thinking he could trick the little people by slipping past them in the darkness. But he did not come home the next day nor the day after. Recognizing the mother's grief would not diminish, and noting the community's desire to find the young man, the elders gathered to create a plan. As they were meeting, a magician came to them and told them he could help them resolve their predicament; he could bring back the much-desired tobacco and, perhaps, find the young man who was lost. They agreed to allow him to try.

This magician was cunning and decided he would turn himself into a mole and tunnel beneath the gorge. Nevertheless, the Yunwi Tsundsdi were clever, too, and they exposed the magician. Irritated, they tracked him down, dragged him out of the ground, and chased him home. Undaunted, the magician turned himself into a tiny hummingbird and flit and flittered his way to the far end of the gorge. It worked! However, he could only bear the weight of a teeny-tiny amount of tobacco with his little wings and wee body. The community was thankful, but many spoke softly about the magician's failure to bring back enough tobacco, nor did he find the young man. Again the magician set out. This time, though, he thought bigger. He turned himself into a torrential whirlwind, spinning and spinning like a tornado through the gorge.

Many trees, shrubs, and boulders were ripped from the mountain in his wake, laying bare the rock cliffs. Exposed, the Yunwi Tsundsdi took their belongings and left their homes there. The magician hastily searched for the young warrior and found little more than bones. Still, he was able to bring him to life. He and the young warrior traveled the gorge and brought back more tobacco than they could hardly carry. Since that time, the Yunwi Tsundsdi are seldom seen within Hickory Nut Gorge, and the Cherokee were able to have plentiful amounts of tobacco.

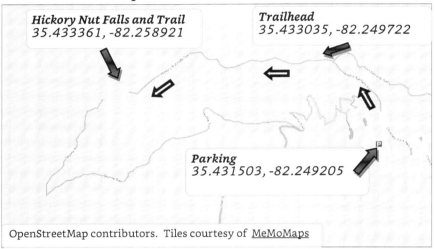

OpenStreetMap contributors. Tiles courtesy of MeMoMaps

Take a hike through Hickory Nut Gorge to a cascading waterfall and watch for any Yunwi Tsundsdi who may have sneaked back into the gorge—

Parking/Trailhead:
Chimney Rock State Park
There is a fee to enter this park.
(35.431503, -82.249205)

Trail: Hickory Nut Falls Trail/Trailhead
Chimney Rock, North Carolina 28720
(35.433035, -82.249722)
Access to the trail is near the Chimney Rock steps past the elevator.
Hike: 0.7 miles, one-way. Hike to Hickory Nut Falls. Trail is easy with some moderate areas. Steps.

The Devil's Courthouse & Tanasee Bald
Transylvania County, North Carolina
Haywood County, North Carolina

The Devil's Courthouse

Devil's Courthouse—It is not difficult to see Tsul'kălû', a slant-eyed giant (also called Judaculla) found here—

Along its 469-mile route, the Blue Ridge Parkway weaves through a subrange of the Blue Ridge Mountains called Great Balsams. Within the Great Balsams, Tanasee Bald and Devil's Courthouse Mountain were a place of legends for the Cherokee living there—that of the Tsul'kălû', a slant-eyed giant who was known for his impressive hunting ability. Tanasee Bald is where Tsul'kălû' cleared land for his home.

And it is the Devil's Courthouse where he danced and held court in an underground cave.

Atop Devil's Courthouse—looking out over the Great Balsams, Tanasee Bald, and the land where Tsul'kălû' roamed.

Many years ago, near Pigeon Gap, there was a Cherokee town called Kanuga. Within this town, there was a widow and her daughter, who was of marriageable age. It was always good for a mother to pass down to her daughters to choose a great hunter among the community for a husband as he would provide sufficient food and a good shelter for the family. This widow did no less for her daughter, reminding her often she must choose such a man.

The daughter lived near her mother's home in an âsï, a dome-shaped winter house made of saplings and mud. One night, a stranger came to the young woman's âsï wishing to court her, but she refused him, saying that her mother would only allow her to marry a great hunter. "I am the great hunter Tsul'kălû'." the stranger replied. So the young woman let him inside, and he stayed the whole night. But before morning came, he said he must take his departure, but he would leave some fine meat for her mother. So when the young woman went outside later in the morning, a huge deer awaited her. She gave it to her mother and told her it was from her sweetheart, which made the widow happy.

On the next night, this hunter returned and left again before daylight. On that morning, he bequeathed two deer, and the mother was even more pleased this time and said to her daughter, "I wish your sweetheart would bring us some wood now." The mysterious stranger could read minds, and the next time he came to the young woman, he told her to tell her mother he had brought wood for her. However, when the mother went out of her home, there were three huge uncut trees, which angered her. She grumbled harshly about the wood being unsplit, and they would have to cut it themselves. The hunter knew the words the woman had harshly spoken, and the next morning when the family awakened, the trees were gone, and there was no wood. The widow had to go to the forest and gather her own kindling.

The hunter continued to visit the young woman, and he would bring deer, yet her mother constantly complained that she would like to meet him. When the young woman asked him to gather with her family, he refused, stating he would frighten them too much. Then his young lover cried until he agreed: "As long as you warn your mother not to say my appearance is frightful," he declared. "I will meet with her." So he did not leave the next morning, and the mother came to visit. When she peered into the âsï, she saw a giant with slanting eyes doubled over resting on the floor with his head against the rafters and toes scraping the roof. One arm rested on one wall while the other rested on the other. She was frightened and began screaming. Her fear angered the hunter; he untwisted himself from the âsï and stated he would never let the mother see him again and would return home to Tsunegun'yi.

While her husband was away, the young woman awakened with her monthly bleeding. There was so much that her mother threw it into the river. One night, after his wife had gone to bed, the hunter returned to the âsï.

He noticed she was alone and asked her where their child had gone. The woman told him there was no child; she had bled, and her mother had thrown the blood into the river. The husband went to the river and found a little worm, which he picked up. As he carried it back to where the young woman lived, it grew and formed into a baby girl. He handed his wife the child and told her she must go live with him as her mother did not like him and abused their child. The wife agreed, and they went to his home.

The young woman had a brother who decided to visit her. He searched for her and followed the giant's footsteps until he found his sister dancing inside a cave on a mountain so steep he could not enter. However, when he called her, she clambered easily along the rock wall with her two children to visit him outside. He came several times, then decided he wanted to meet her husband. But the giant said, "You cannot see me until you put on a new dress." And the young man agreed. The giant then declared that he would allow all of Kanuga to meet him, but the brother had to return to his people and tell them that they must go to the townhouse (a council house or central house used for meetings). "Tell them within the townhouse that they must fast for seven days. They cannot come out of the townhouse in those seven days. They must not raise a war whoop. And on the seventh day, I will bring new dresses for you to wear so that you can all see me."

The brother returned to Kanuga and told the people what the giant told him, and they all wanted to see Tsul'kălû'. So all the community of Kanuga entered the townhouse and fasted for seven days, except for one warrior who had stolen in from another settlement and then snuck out each night to eat before slipping back in again.

On the seventh day, when the sun rose around the townhouse, those within heard a great thunder come near.

As scared as the community was when the noise grew louder, they each held their breath and made no sound. That is, except for the man who snuck into Kanuga and did not fast. In great fear, he ran outside and cried a war whoop. Then, suddenly, there was silence as if whatever made the sound was moving far away. The people went out, and it appeared nothing had changed; the land was just as it had been seven days earlier.

Undaunted, the brother would return to see his sister. "Why did Tsul'kălû' not bring the dresses as he promised?" he asked his sister. And from somewhere above, a great voice rumbled, "I brought the dresses, but you did not do as I told you. Instead, you broke the fast and raised a war whoop." The young man said, "It was not those of our community, but one who snuck in. We will come again and do as you say." But Tsul'kălû' only replied, "Now you will never see me." And the young man could say no more and returned to Kanuga.

The trail to Devil's Courthouse is well-maintained and short, but also a strenuous climb at points.

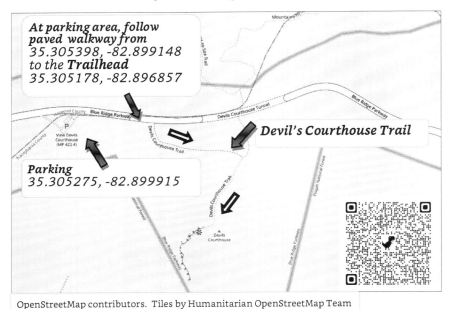

Follow the trail to the top of Devil's Courthouse, a lair of the Tsul'kălû', and view the Balsam Mountains where his feet once tread.

Parking/Trailhead:
Devil's Courthouse Parking Area
MP 422.4, Blue Ridge Pkwy
Balsam Grove, North Carolina 28708
(35.305275, -82.899915)

Trail: Devil's Courthouse Overlook

Trailhead: (35.305178, -82.896857)

Overlook: (35.302970, -82.895916)

Hike: 0.5 miles, one-way. Out and back. Access the trail by a paved walkway paralleling the Blue Ridge Parkway for a short distance. Mid to strenuous hike. Steps. Mostly paved and short, but some may find the climb challenging.

Great Smoky Mountains National Park
Noland Creek Trail
Swain County, North Carolina

Ghost Town

Along Noland Creek and the trail—

Old ghost town cemeteries hidden beneath thickly forested hillocks, abandoned homesteads waiting evermore for their owners to return, and ghostly and disturbing lore surround the Noland Creek Trail in the Smoky Mountains about 8 miles from Bryson City. Even a dark Cherokee legend crosses its path—

Spearfinger—Many years ago, in the heads of streams in the Smoky Mountains, there was a horrible ogress that Cherokee called her "U'tlun'ta," One With Pointed Spear or Spearfinger. Spearfinger's entire body was covered in stone-like skin that no weapon could pierce, and she had the power to take the shape of anything she preferred.

The forefinger of her right hand was long and as skinny as a sharp knife, and her favorite prey were young children. If she heard them playing outside their camp, she would take the form of an old woman and follow their sweet scent, hobbling as if she was having great difficulty walking. "I am tired," she would say, sitting beside them as if wanting to watch them play. Then with her speared-finger hand hidden in her dress, she would call out to one of them. "Come sit on grandma's lap, and I will sing you a song and play with your hair." And one of them would come skipping and prancing over and plop their little head happily on her lap in anticipation of the special attention.

U'tlun'ta crooned and cooed over the child and slipped her fingers through its hair until the child fell into a blissful nap. Then, U'tlun'ta whipped her hand from its hidden pocket in her clothing, sinking the speared forefinger through the tender flesh of the back of the child's neck until the tip pierced its liver. She would drag out the liver and eat it as it dripped with blood, smacking her lips and sighing contentedly while the other children ran screeching away.

The Bobbing Lantern—That Spearfinger might hobble up in the form of an old woman and greet the unwary hiker is not the only concern when taking the trail. After the Native Americans roamed this area, settlers moved into the lush forest along the steady creek and built homes—living and dying, and some of their offspring would later work in the lumber yards that sprang up in the late 1800s and early 1900s along the creek there.

The remains of a Noland Creek home along the trail. In the 1930s, after lumbering battered the countryside, a wealthy man named Philip Rust bought over 4,300 acres along Noland Creek for reforestation in the Solola area. He built a summer cottage for himself, a nurse's home, a pottery building for his wife, and other structures, including a waterwheel-powered turbine. He hired locals to care for the property year-round. These are the ruins of a 7-room home where the estate warden Cole Hyatt lived with his family until the Tennessee Valley Authority forced those in the area to vacate for Lake Fontana projects.

The house fell into decay in the 1950s after vacating and before razing.

One early settler's daughter disappeared into the woods one late afternoon. By dusk, she had not returned, so her father lit a lantern and rambled into the oncoming darkness with his light held high over his head, calling her name.

He walked the creek shore for hours until he decided to expand his search area outside the safe and easy-to-follow border of Noland Creek. He went long past the deep of night, refusing to turn around until he found her. Louder his calls became the farther he wandered into the deep forest. But she was nowhere to be found. Finally, he became disoriented, and many times, he struggled to retrace his steps, but he grasped too late that he was lost. He would continue into the next day and then the night, calling out for her until he perhaps decided to rest and lay down and die, disappearing into the fold of the forest just like his daughter, never to return. Nobody ever found the man or his daughter. However, some have witnessed his lantern light bobbing along in the darkness of the Smoky Mountains. And the old man has been known to guide lost hikers back to the Noland Creek Trail, once a Native Indian path and later, a rugged roadway.

From about 1880 to 1911, lumber mill towns popped up along Forney and Noland Creek, and it was quite a busy place. Above, a slab camp at Forney Creek was set up where wood was prepared for sawing into planks. Image: NPS

More Mysterious Disappearances and Murders—If that is not enough to frighten those hiking the trail, there have been many disturbing disappearances and mysterious deaths in the area beginning over a hundred years ago. In November of 1911, a man hunting chestnuts discovered a desiccated corpse secreted beneath logs and planks in a remote area near Noland Creek Trail. No one knew his identity, although a stranger had stopped into Bryson and stayed at a local hotel only a few months earlier. The clothing he wore was like that of the dead man. He had asked about purchasing some lands with minerals, inquiring about the location of the head of Noland Creek. He never returned, and law enforcement did not find his identity or solve the murder.

For quite some time, many believed the body was that of John Hunter of Mill Creek, not too far away, who had disappeared from his home in 1909. His family searched for years for Mister Hunter, but it was not until 1922 when some lumbermen were cutting down Chestnut trees a mile and a half from his home that they discovered bones within a tree with a hollow base. The remains were shoved head-first about ten feet up into the trunk and sealed carefully with mud and dirt. His grandson tried to determine if it was his grandfather with the skull found, but without fillings present or enough of the skull to recognize, the family could not distinguish if it was John Hunter.

Disappearances—About 13 miles, as the crow flies, away from the head of Noland Creek Trail, on June 14, 1969, 6-year-old Dennis Martin was on the family's traditional Father's Day weekend camping trip to the Great Smoky Mountains National Park. He was with his 9-year-old brother Douglas, his father, a Knoxville architect, and grandfather, a teacher. There was also another family traveling with them.

Dennis was a happy little fellow with a mop of dark brown hair, brown eyes, and a partial toothless grin. While hiking and camping, they stopped at Spence Field along the Appalachian Trail. Dennis, Douglas, and the other children decided to play a prank by splitting off by the trail and jumping out at the adults when they passed them. As planned, the children jumped out; however, Dennis did not appear. Growing concerned after a five-minute lapse, Dennis's father ran along the trail looking for the little boy. After several hours, they were able to contact a park ranger. A search was immediately made, including park rangers, volunteers, the FBI, and the National Guard. Unfortunately, nobody has ever found a trace of Dennis and he is still missing.

On Friday morning, October 8, 1976, 16-year-old brown-haired, green-eyed Trenny Gibson was on a class field trip to the Smoky Mountains with her high school horticulture class from Bearden High in Knoxville, Tennessee. Although it was a chilly, drizzly day, she only wore a blue blouse, pale blue striped sweater, and blue jeans. After the bus was parked at Clingman's Dome, the teacher told the students that their assignment was to hike to Andrew's Bald, a 1.8-mile (one-way) hike, then meet back at the bus at 3:30 p.m. They were allowed to set their own pace, and the teacher followed along on the trail, mingling with the students as they walked. Trenny buddied up with an old friend named Robert to Andrew's Bald, where they stopped to eat lunch. On the return, she headed alone along the trail and ahead of Robert toward the bus, but not before she borrowed his orange plaid woolen jacket as she was getting cold.

At one point, on her return to the bus and at a hurried pace, she passed several other students. It was at a spot on the trail not far after, and from a distance, students saw her peering into the woods before she vanished from sight.

When the students passed this place, there was no sign of Trenny. Instead, they saw thick shrubs and a ridge they thought nobody could ramble through easily and as quickly as they had caught up to the last place they saw her. Still, a few called out for their schoolmate. She did not answer. And when the bus readied to leave, Trenny Gibson was not to be found. There was a massive search for the girl with helicopters, rescuers on the ground, and teams of search dogs. Law enforcement found no trace of her, and Trenny is still missing.

The Smoky Mountains have long been a place of mystery and wild beauty. Walking Noland Creek Trail nowadays is like taking a mystical step back in time—along the trail are the remains of old buildings, many sadly leftover from the forced departure of families in the area when the government built the national park and Lake Fontana. There are cemeteries, too, tucked into the mountainsides. These old villages of the dead have become the silent reminders that real families like yours and mine lived, loved, laughed, cried, and died along the banks of Noland Creek. And sometimes, passed their ghost stories and folk tales along—

A bridge along the path—

Hike to Upper and Lower Noland Creek Cemeteries—

Check out a couple of ghost towns in the Smoky Mountains.

Parking/Trailhead:
Bryson City, North Carolina 28713
(35.457532, -83.526724)
There is a small sign at the parking trailhead (If back is to Lakeview Drive, it is to the right. There is also a secondary trail to the left with a short walkway parallel to Lakeview Drive.) Follow the trail to the base of the hill, where hikers will see Noland Creek (35.457592, -83.527307).

Hike: Total about 4.5 miles, one-way, which includes the two cemetery spur trails. Out and back. Easy (main trail along an old roadbed) to moderate (rugged, dirt cemetery trails up steeper hillsides).

The hike is along an old roadbed passing ruins of homes in the community. It parallels Noland Creek with two mountain spur trails with cemetery stops along the way:

1) Lower Noland-Monteith Cemetery

2) Upper Noland Branton Creek Cemetery.

Take a right. Pass underneath the Lakeview Drive viaduct and then *the first wooden bridge*. Hikers will pass Bearpen Branch Backcountry Campsite (#65) on the left at 1.2 miles from the viaduct where the Noland Creek School was located. In about 0.5 miles, there is an abandoned farm field and a second wooden bridge. Watch for ruins of a few old homesteads in this area along the 0.4 miles.

1) **Lower Noland Monteith Cemetery** — *0.3 miles, one-way. Out and back. Moderately Steep. (35.486440, -83.509390)*

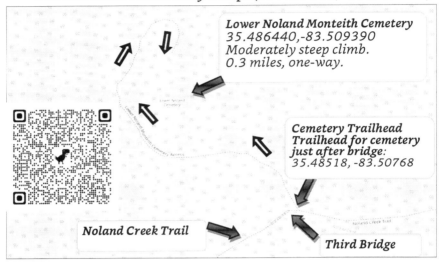

After hikers cross the third wooden bridge, the trail intersects (on the left) a rugged dirt path to **Lower Noland-Monteith Cemetery** (35.48518, -83.50768). Take this left after *the third bridge on the Noland Creek Trail*. There is a sign with "no horse traffic" marking the trail.

Lower Noland-Monteith Cemetery—

After returning to the Noland Creek Trail, continue into the Solola Valley before passing the Mill Creek Backcountry Campsite (#64) (35.49770, -83.50189) at about 1.4 miles from the cemetery access. Mill Creek School was once located here, along with homes in the 1930s.

2) Upper Noland Creek Cemetery—*0.2 miles, one-way. Out and back. (35.49618, -83.49877)*

Just beyond, hikers will cross a log footbridge over Noland Creek. In 0.2 miles, an access trail leads to Philip Rust's home and, following wooden steps, to the Upper Noland Cemetery.

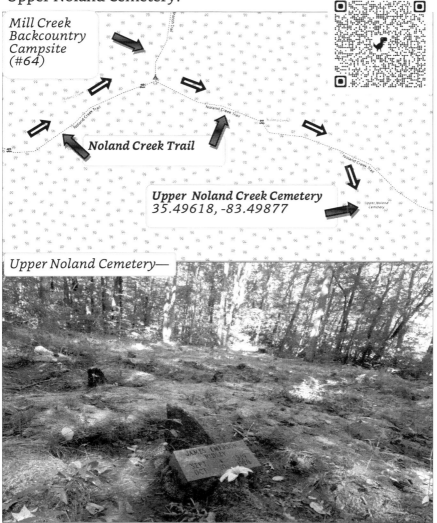

Upper Noland Cemetery—

Before hiking to the cemetery (via steps to the left in the image below), look to the right. This area is the location of Philip Rust's summer home. It is hard to believe there was once a beautiful family summer cottage in this location (circa the 1930s), more cottages for close family friends, and even a dwelling for a nurse. There was also a pottery kiln for Rust's wife, sheep, equestrian barns, and a trout farm! Those with a keen eye might even see the remains of a waterwheel-powered turbine used to run the estate.

Area of the old estate today—

Philip Rust's abandoned summer home in the 1950s after being forced to give up the property. NPS.org

Virginia

Shenandoah National Park—Upper Pocosin Mission Greene County, Virginia

The Abandoned Old Pocosin Mission

Ruins of the Old Pocosin Mission along the Appalachian Trail.

From the 1700s to the early 1900s, many small communities popped up on the land now the Shenandoah National Park. Families lived in the hundreds of homes scattered along the countryside of the Blue Ridge Mountains. When it came to the attention of Episcopalian minister Frederick William Neve in the late 1800s that these remote areas had no educational or religious facilities, he began preaching throughout these isolated pockets.

He also brought the stories of those living within to other Episcopalians, and such, the church developed missions or outposts with schools and churches that also provided food and clothing to those in need.

The French Memorial Chapel at Upper Pocosin Mission around 1920. Image: University of Virginia Special Collections. Blue Ridge Missions, Diocese of Virginia.

One of those missions established in 1908 in a deep hollow of the mountains was Upper Pocosin Episcopal Mission. This mission had several buildings, including a rough-hewn log and frame cabin to house workers and a church with weekly Sunday services that also doubled as a school five days a week. Christians Florence and Marion Towles were missionaries at Pocosin for many years when the mission was present. Although they would later say the time spent there was the happiest of their lives, it was not without its hardships. The land was isolated, and the two did not understand the local ways of life. The winters were harsh, and the summers hot. Their cabin was scanty, and where the two sisters lived, moonshine flowed freely among some rougher crowds within the region, and the rowdiness of those who imbibed frightened the devout sisters.

School and Mission Cabin—Image: University of Virginia Special Collections. Blue Ridge Missions, Diocese of Virginia.

The Pocosin Community lasted into the 1930s until the families around it were forced to vacate along with thousands of others to make way for the creation of Shenandoah National Park. However, some things from this abandoned ghost town endure for hikers to witness. A stone church built by Billy Graves, a local mason, is nearly gone, but the old steps leading into the building remain, and a sagging wooden structure barely clings to life. Some have even walked the path to the old mission and remarked about hearing voices or odd sounds. Yet no one else is around!

Members of the community—Image: University of Virginia Special Collections. Blue Ridge Missions, Diocese of Virginia.

The trail is well-maintained and an easy hike—

A family in the Upper Pocosin community—Image: University of Virginia Special Collections. Blue Ridge Missions, Diocese of Virginia.

The stone steps once leading to the mission's church—

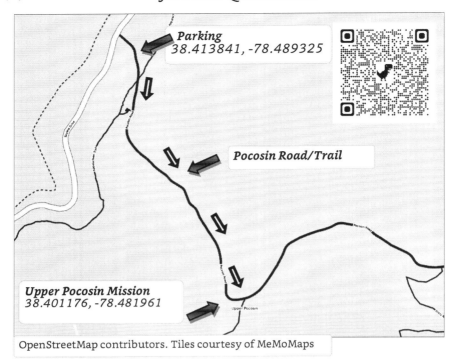

OpenStreetMap contributors. Tiles courtesy of MeMoMaps

Hike to the abandoned Pocosin Mission—

Parking/Trailhead: Around mile 59.5 on Skyline Drive, a gravel road leads to a small parking area.
(38.413841, -78.489325)

Hike: (38.413583, -78.488969) 1.0 miles, one-way. Out and back. At the far end of the parking area are two yellow posts and a chain to stop traffic from continuing; this marks the beginning of the trail, which will intersect and follow the Appalachian Trail. Follow the old roadbed, and at mile 0.2, you will pass one of the Potomac Appalachian Trail Club's cabin rentals, a CCC cabin built in the 1930s for use as housing during the construction of Skyline Drive. Continue downward along the gentle descent about 0.8 miles to Upper Pocosin Mission. You will easily see the old ruins of a wooden building and the church steps. There is a gradual downhill grade to the location.

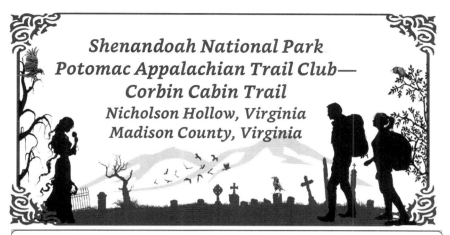

Shenandoah National Park Potomac Appalachian Trail Club— Corbin Cabin Trail
Nicholson Hollow, Virginia
Madison County, Virginia

The Old Haunted Cabin in the Woods

An old cabin is tucked deep in a hollow within Shenandoah National Park. It is haunted. Hikers can take the 1.4-mile trek to it and stay the night if they dare. I did.

There is an old cabin tucked deep in the woods of Shenandoah National Park, nearly a mile and a half down a narrow, steep trail beneath a canopy of mature trees and across a bubbling river. It rests there with an occasional rattlesnake sunning itself on a boulder a few steps away. Once in a while, a deer, bear, or raccoon ambles past, doing what wild animals do in the wild—foraging for food, searching for a mate, or seeking a place to rest their heads.

It is the George T. Corbin Cabin, and I try to get back there yearly for a stay.

It was a dry autumn when I backpacked in this last time, and the Hughes River I had to cross was hardly running. The spring was dried up, and the air was about 70 degrees during the day. However, the weather took a turn soon enough. It dipped down to 20-30 degrees at night. It was as if Mother Nature suddenly realized that it was time to escort the seemingly long, carefree autumn out to allow the angrier winter to stomp in. The wind kicked up in the hollow in the dark evening air, knocking and banging the trees outside and making moaning noises sweep up through the forest. I did not light a fire; I just hunkered down in the kitchen in my sleeping bag. It was quiet in the cabin until I was gently goaded from sleep by occasional deep coughing.

On a cold night, the kitchen near the stove was the warmer place to stay. Here, I slept and listened to the sounds of ghostly footsteps and occasional coughs.

Once, footsteps resounded in the other room as if someone was quietly going about some task. I did not rise on either occasion. I knew the cabin was haunted by those who previously lived within its walls. That night, they were quiet. Oh, but it was not that way the first time I visited the cabin. Nope, not at all. But it makes sense because *then* I was an unexpected guest. And folks, whether alive or dead, do not always take to strangers dropping in uninvited, building a fire in their kitchen stove, eating at their table, and camping out on their floor. So let me tell you my ghost story about me barging into Mister George Corbin's home my first time without as much as a knock on the door. Nobody quietly tiptoed around the stranger so as not to awaken her that time. Instead, I was greeted more appropriately by a family who appeared slightly annoyed at the uninvited guest.

4.0 miles from the trailhead for Corbin Cabin—The summit of Stony Man overlooking Shenandoah National Park. **Trailhead Parking to Summit and Trailhead:** (No pets) Hike: 0.7 miles, out and back. Off Skyland Upper Loop. (38.593189, -78.375737)

Stony Man is the second-highest mountain in Shenandoah National Park. The Hughes River flows from its slopes, down and deep, to a valley called Nicholson Hollow, now a remote forest. However, it was not always secluded.

This hollow was home to a community of homesteaders who lived by farming, grazing, apple growing, and distilling. George Corbin resided there, a mountain farmer who built a cabin when he was 21-years- old by the Hughes River. It was close to his father's home. George's place was two stories with a single living room downstairs and a single upstairs room and the perfect place to live, love, and raise a family.

George would live most of his life in the hollow. He married three times; his first wife Mildred died before he built the cabin, and his second wife Bertie passed away in the home in February of 1924, only three hours after the birth of their third child. As years passed, George added a kitchen and other areas to his cabin; he married Eula Nicholson, then in the 1930s, the Corbin family was forced to vacate as the land was going to be a part of the Shenandoah National Park.

The George Corbin Cabin—

The historic cabin is one of the few that somehow survived the demolition of many homesteads in the park.

Now the volunteer group Potomac Appalachian Club does an incredible job of maintaining and renting out the Corbin Cabin as one of 43 cabins so folks can get a taste of history, enjoy the outdoors, and experience what it was like to live in the mountains in earlier years. I had heard the old cabin was haunted, but the stories were vague. Some believe it is George's dead wife, Bertie, who comes back and makes a racket when folks visit. It was a cold winter's day when she passed after giving birth to their child. The doctor had come to check on the new mother and driven to the closest road. George had waited for him on the path to his home with his horse and brought the man down. All seemed fine with the birth, but when George returned from taking the doctor to his vehicle, he found his wife lifeless. He buried her in the frozen ground of the cemetery near the house, then walked four hours to Nethers to get the baby's milk. Is it she who makes a ghostly presence? Or is it the groans of an old home making noises, the bangs of a nosy wild animal bumping around the building, or the babbling creek chattering?

Nethers, Virginia, around the time of the Great Depression—where Mister Corbin trudged through the snow to get milk for the baby.

I decided I wanted to find out. The first time I visited, I went in mid-November. Those who know me understand I am not a "ghost hunter" who goes out antagonizing ghosts with rude confrontations and loads of newfangled equipment. I like the folklore, the stories, and sitting back and letting spirits come to me if they wish. And occasionally, they do. Often, I have found that this approach and just a camera and digital recorder make for more encounters. However, I will admit that fiddling with all the scientific equipment is just fun.

Some of the families of Corbin and Nicholson Hollows—Library of Congress

George Corbin who built the cabin. Taken from picture in the cabin.

Regardless, I do not know why I picked that time of year; I do not particularly like camping or renting a non-electric cabin in the winter. The only heat available at Corbin Cabin is a pot-belly stove that needs to be fed wood all night and barely warms a small kitchen area. But after a drive, with backpack tossed over my shoulders, hand warmers tucked into my pocket, and a flashlight, I headed out.

Getting to Corbin Cabin from the parking area is along the same rugged trail that early homesteaders busted through the mountain, so it is narrow, rocky, and wild, and straight down on the way to the cabin and narrow and straight up on the way out. And at the trail's end, hikers must cross the modest Hughes River by a series of stepping stones before getting to the cabin. In the dark, I fumbled around on the trail, traversed the water without incident, and even saw a bear before it saw me and ran off into the forest.

The trail crossing at the Hughes River with the cabin just beyond—

Once inside, I set my flashlight on the floor and laid my sleeping bag on a couple of blankets right in front of the stove. To set the mood for the cabin stay, I played some old Bluegrass songs while I got warm. Finally, I went to bed at about 9:00 or 10:00 in the silent and dark air. There were no lights but the meager fire, and just as I laid down, I saw a shadow like a man leaning against the doorway between the two rooms, and a voice said quite clearly: "Dee, I think we've got company."

I shot up, thinking for a half-second that I'd gone to the wrong cabin, then quickly remembered I had a key that unlocked it. I was not scared, just startled. I lay there for a while, stoked the fire, and fell deep asleep. (And by the way, I was not sure who "Dee" was when I heard the voice. But it was clearly that name.)

Sometime during the night, I was awakened by: "Ma'am?" I worked my way up on my elbow, thinking I had dreamed of hearing the voice. I noticed the fire was out, and it was chilly, so I added some more wood. There was a lot of banging going on outside, which I figured was a bear as it was too large for raccoons, so I laid back down and enjoyed the bumps and bangs of the woods until I fell asleep.

I cannot remember the time of night when I captured this picture. But, obviously, from my snarky smile and stink eye, it was when my patience for ghosts was running thin. Upper left—you can see an image of a ghostly figure at the doorway.

Again, I was awakened by a chill in the air, and "Ma'am?" I opened my eyes, looked around, and realized I must have fallen asleep for a couple of hours; the fire was out again.

I stoked it up and tried to fall back asleep. Now it was really cold out that night and dark. I walked to the outhouse outside with my cell phone light blazing and did not see anything amiss. I returned and was fully awake from the brisk walk, and as I lay there, it sounded like three or four people were trekking past the cabin. I looked at the time, and it was about 2:00 in the morning. I thought it odd that someone was hiking this late in the dark on a 4 to 5-mile loop trail, but I listened to their chatter for the longest time, and then they faded away.

So, the night progressed as such—each time the fire went out, I was awakened by that "Ma'am?" I would estimate it was 4 or 6 times. Had the voice not roused me in the fifteen-degree night, I would have been darn frozen when I awakened in the morning. But it did. And I stayed cozy and warm all night.

I assume Mister Corbin haunts the home, and I appreciated his gesture in not allowing me to freeze to death that night. Those who knew George Corbin said he was a pleasant and friendly man. I think that perhaps he was caring too. And I am glad he and his family were kind enough to share his old homestead with me, this stranger who made herself comfortable within without an invitation from them on more than one occasion. Perhaps he will welcome you too.

**Parking: Corbin Cabin Cutoff Parking
Shenandoah National Park**

Parking: Skyline Drive (The Skyline Drive is the 105-mile scenic road through the Shenandoah National Park)
Luray, Virginia 22835
(38.615810, -78.350587)
You can rent the cabin or hike the trail to the cabin.
There is a fee to get into the park.

Trailhead: To get to the trailhead, you must walk directly across Skyline Drive. Trailhead is marked by a cement post.
(38.615624, -78.350466)

Here are two options for hiking the trail. Both have the same parking/trailhead.

1) Hike to Corbin Cabin Out and Back

2) Hike Corbin Cabin Hollow, Nicholson Hollow, and Appalachian Trail Loop Trail

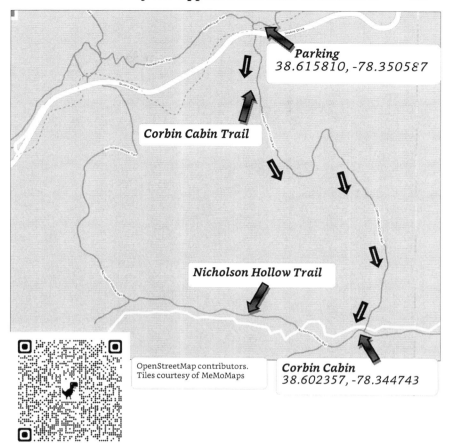

Hike to Corbin Cabin and visit the Corbin Family:

Parking/Trailhead: (Corbin Cabin Cutoff Trail) 1.4 miles, one-way. Out and back. Steep. All downhill to the Corbin Cabin on a dirt path and a strenuous hike back out to the parking lot. Thick woodland. To get to the cabin, hikers will need to cross Hughes River, a small stream, by jumping boulders which, seasonally, may flow rapidly. (38.615810, -78.350587)

Cabin: (38.602357, -78.344743) The trail passes the cabin. The Potomac Appalachian Club rents the building to visitors, so please be courteous and respect the privacy of those staying there.

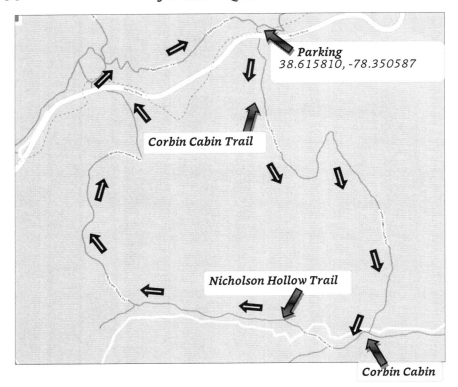

Hike Corbin Cabin Hollow, Nicholson Hollow, and Appalachian Trail Loop Trail

Hike: 4.2 miles. Loop. Hikers continue along Nicholson Hollow Trail for a loop trail back to the Corbin Cutoff Parking Area. To get to the cabin, hikers will need to cross Hughes River, a small stream, by jumping boulders which, seasonally, may flow rapidly.

After crossing the Hughes River (on the cabin side), hikers will see the Nicholson Hollow Trail. The climb back toward Skyline Drive is steep before reaching the road. Take a left on Skyline Drive for about 70-75 yards. Hikers will note a spur trail leading to the Appalachian Trail, marked by a cement post. Go right, for 0.5 miles, to the parking lot.

The Killing Rock Massacre

The journey from Cane Creek Branch to the community of Pound through Pound Gap and up Pine Mountain would be the last time one moonshining man and his family would travel together.

The Pound Gap is a high, natural pass that runs along the Virginia and Kentucky borders between Pound, Virginia and the head of Elkhorn Creek in Jenkins, Kentucky. It offered a way for explorers and settlers to cross Pine Mountain from Virginia and into Kentucky as a path of less resistance.

During the Civil War, Confederate and Union troops used the gap as it was easy access into Kentucky, giving rise to a few battles for this pass. One included Union General James Garfield and his troops' defeat of the Confederates in March of 1862. In 1864, Confederate John Hunt Morgan was able to force a Union detachment from Pound Gap. It was also used by those living in the small communities surrounding it to travel from one town to the next. And one family would take the journey from Clear Creek Branch, Kentucky (now Jenkins) to Pound, Virginia, and it would be the last time they would travel together again.

A revenue man discovering a moonshine still—

Thirty-five-year-old Ira Mullins was a farmer and merchant with a side-job of moonshining (producing) and bootlegging (selling) illegal alcohol in the mountains of eastern Kentucky and western Virginia. He often clashed with the revenue agents enforcing the bootlegging laws.

One of the revenue agents that he came into contact with was Marshall Benton Taylor who deplored those who broke the liquor laws and if he felt slighted by something, he held a grudge. Taylor would sneak around and use a long spyglass to stake out possible moonshine stills and their peddlers as part of one job, arresting or shooting at those he caught depending upon his mood on a certain day. There was also talk he was part of a vigilante group for timber and coal companies, paid large sums of money to intimidate small landowners into giving up their property.

Known as "Doc Taylor," he had no formal medical education. He received tutelage from an uncle for a short period on doctoring and herbs. He was a self-proclaimed preacher with a past, accused of murdering an outlaw in cold blood in his own home and in front of the man's wife. He was acquitted and later became a deputy. During his duties, he was part of a posse that captured a wagon load of whiskey driven through the town of Wise Courthouse. It was Ira Mullins' wagon that placed the man in Taylor's eyeshot because Taylor lost his U.S. Marshall's job due to the incident on the grounds his bosses believed he was unstable. Even worse, after that, Taylor held a grudge against Ira Mullins to the point he became fixated on hunting down and killing the man. It did not help, too, that Taylor was good friends with Mullins' neighbor, Henry Vanover. He and Ira had been feuding for quite some time over ownership of their abutting properties.

During one flight from the revenue agents, Ira Mullins was shot, leaving him paralyzed and unable to walk or feed himself. At some point after, an unknown assailant shot straight through his bedroom window into his bed. The bullet barely missed Mullins and caught his bedclothes and mattress on fire. He knew both Vanover and Doc Taylor loathed him, and the gunman was most likely one of them.

Rumors began to arise that several moonshine peddlers, including Ira Mullins (who could not seek revenge as he was bedridden), were planning Doc Taylor's death and offering a reward for the revenuer's head of $300.00, which did not fare well with the other man.

Fearing for his life, Ira Mullins rounded up his family to stay with the Wilson Mullins family, in-laws at the mouth of Cane Creek Branch, near present-day Jenkins, Kentucky. However, after they were there a while, they decided to return home to Pound, Virginia, to get some belongings. A party of eight started off the early morning of May 14, 1892. The travelers became one less when the family left Wilson's 11-year-old daughter Mindy with her grandmother. The little girl was so visibly upset she did not get to tag along that her father bought her a can of sweet peaches, opened them, then let her feast upon them to cheer her up. Before he left, he told her he would be back soon. That would not come to pass.

Along the trail on the Virginia side, a watering trough for horses along the old route—

They set off across the mountain by way of the rough roads of Pound Gap on an old trace called Fincastle Trail. The family had loaded Ira into the back of a wagon. He was partially sitting up, lying on a pallet with hay atop for comfort from the jars of the wagon on the rutted path. His wife Louranza, 32 years old, was beside him with nearly a thousand dollars in their life savings tucked into her undergarments. A hired hand with limited intelligence, 13-year-old John Chappel was driving the two-horse wagon. Ira's 14-year-old son John Harrison walked with 14-year-old Greenberry Harris just behind. Wilson Mullins and his wife, Jane, had come along to help. Wilson walked before the wagon, and Jane was on horseback.

It was a steady, rough, uphill climb with some areas almost too slim for a wagon to fit—

It was a slow climb up the northwestern slope of Pine Mountain, on a trail called Pine Mountain Trail within Pound Gap, with a few stops along the way to rest. By noon they had arrived at Pound Gap and began to descend along the Fincastle Trail toward Pound, Virginia. It was a warm day, and the leaves were starting to show on the trees. Birds chirped above, and the wind whistled softly along the trail.

Abruptly, an explosion of gunshot blasted into the air, issued from a pile of boulders near the side of the trail where three men with masks covering their faces had been hiding in wait to ambush the family.

Within seconds while the air filled with the reek of the gunshot, Ira Mullins lay dead with eight shots to his body. His wife was fired upon in the breast and knees and died shortly after. The two wagon horses died with a few more blasts. Wilson ducked for cover, and the villains shot him dead. Jane was thrown from her panicked horse, and the frightened beast headed into the woods. Two children, John Chappel and Greenberry Harris, were shot in the head and body. The massacre did not last long. Five lay dead. Two escaped—Jane Mullins and 14-year-old John Harrison Mullins, who ran to Kentucky holding his pants up with both hands so they did not fall to his ankles. His suspenders were nearly cut in half by a bullet in his flight to escape. The family's money was taken from Louranza's satchel hidden in her underclothes and her dress thrown up over her head.

The Killing Rock—where the murderers hid—

Jane Mullins saw the killers. She identified them as Marshall Benton Taylor, Calvin Fleming, and Samuel Fleming. Eventually, Taylor was caught and sentenced to death. Before execution, his wife made him a white suit and white cap for his hanging, and he was allowed to preach at his funeral. He also asked that his corpse be kept in his coffin for three days before burial, for he stated that on the third day, he would rise from death to preach again.

On October 27, 1893, the sheriff let him stand at the courthouse's upstairs window, read from the bible, and lead a short sermon to the curious crowd in the courtyard who had come to enjoy a good hanging, as hangings were quite an event at the time. Taylor and his wife Nancy partook in communion, asking if anyone wanted to join them. No one came forth. And so Marshall Benton Taylor was hanged. His family laid his corpse in a coffin for three days. He failed to rise from the dead and was buried in Wise Cemetery.

Calvin Flemings fled after the murders, but bounty hunters killed him in 1894. Samuel Fleming got away. Many believe that Jane Mullins was murdered a few years later, so she could not testify in Samuel's court hearing. She died when a gun was fired into her kitchen window. And on a small trail atop Pine Mountain at Pound Gap, hikers can walk to a monument that stands near some boulders to show where a family was brutally massacred. It is called Killing Rock. And some say, the ghost of Marshall Benton Taylor, who was later dubbed "Red Fox" for his red hair and conniving character, still lurks in the shadows of the mountains of Kentucky and Virginia, waiting for someone to cross his path.

Family and close neighbors recovered the bodies of the five murder victims and laid them out inside Wilson and Jane's home and on the porch while a fire was built to keep away the insects. After the watch and visitation, they were buried at the Potter Family Cemetery in Jenkins, Kentucky. However, on August 15, 1892, the Richmond Virginia Dispatch wrote an article, *Ghouls Dynamite Remains*. "The grave of Ira Mullins, the man who was murdered near Pound Gap last spring, has lately been desecrated in an inhuman manner. Some ghoulish wretches blew the grave up with dynamite or some other explosive substance, exposing the remains of the murdered man. In life, he had some terrible enemies and their vengeance is not yet satisfied—"

Today, the cemetery is quiet. Nobody bothers the graves, and those beneath do not rise; they sleep even if their murderer does not. The Letcher County Historical Society has placed stones upon the five graves. The top stone states: *Killing Rock Massacre. 5 People Killed. Jenkins Mountain. 5-14-1892.*

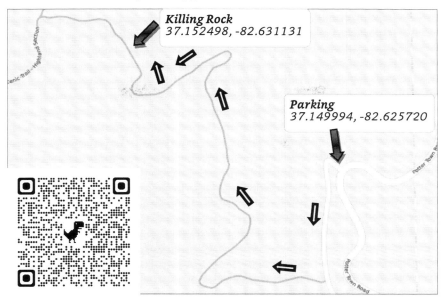

Hike to Killing Rock—Pound Gap Massacre Site:
Parking/Trailhead:
12245 Potter Town Road
Pound, Virginia 24279
(37.149994, -82.625720) The parking lot is a small gravel pull-off at the trailhead. After a forestry gate, hikers will see the first sign, "Red Fox," presenting the trail.

Hike: Killing Rock Site: (37.152498, -82.631131)
0.9 miles, one-way. Well-marked with yellow blazes. Out and back. The course starts on an old gravel road. Hikers follow easy-to-see wooden signs that state, "Red Fox Trail." (The trail was named for the murderer Marshall Benton Taylor who was called "Red Fox" for his red hair and wily character.) Then, it turns off the gravel road to the right (blocked for traffic by an orange USDA Forest Service gate) and continues via a worn dirt trail to the site. It is gentle but moderately strenuous uphill on the way there and downhill on the return. There are a couple of easy creeks to jump over seasonally and fascinating signs about historical places along the way. This particular path became one of my favorite journeys. It offered everything I like in a trail. It had a well-marked route in great condition, entertaining interpretive signs, yet fun and invigorating with different surroundings and trail bases (creek crossings, old roadway, typical dirt path, and thick forest). Oh, and a ghost, as I was quite clearly asked along the route, "Hey, what you doing?"

Gravel pull-off parking—The trail begins with a sign just past the forestry gate.

Interpretive sign showing the location that "One-eye Dock" Mullins would haul cars through a narrow, soggy pass for a small fee.

The Killing Rock, center, and interpretive sign.

And while you are there—check out the Shadow Stealer—

The Chesapeake and Ohio railroad once had a tunnel that connected Pound, Virginia, with Jenkins, Kentucky. It was built to open up a huge coal mine field. From what I gathered, it ran deep into the mountain and was ¾ of a mile long, only supported by timber on the Virginia side, and always collapsing because workers hit a coal seam while developing it. The tunnel closed, partly due to safety concerns, by 1958. The walls and roof were caving in.

Tall grasses almost obliterate the railbed, but the tunnel still exists, and above it, "1947 PINE MOUNTAIN TUNNEL" is marked in concrete. Something lurks within the tunnel. Those who stand outside have seen darkness move within, and it is believed to steal people's shadows. That said, please do not go inside this tunnel. It is not safe. Not simply because there is something creepy within but because you might die if the roof collapses. You can access a path to the tunnel by turning right just past the first forestry gate at the parking lot and turning right at the sign that states: RED FOX TRAIL. After that, you have to forge through tall grasses and muck.

Combs Overlook
View of Raven Rock
Letcher County, Kentucky
(Placed with the Virginia stories as it is right up the street from the Red Fox Trail)

Bobbing Lantern Light

View from Combs Overlook—Take a quick stop off the highway at Combs Overlook to stretch your legs, and you might see a ghost.

During the Civil War, there were a few battles between Confederate and Union troops trying to maintain control or gain access to the strategically important Pound Gap, with its well-trod trails and gateway between Kentucky and Virginia. Soldiers would keep watch on a well-known rock outcropping above Jenkins as the view covered great distances and offered an extensive vantage point.

One soldier has never left his post there. Since the end of the war, those traveling along the roads and paths around Raven Rock have seen a lantern light bobbing and swaying about and can make out the form of a soldier standing there, even when nobody living is near the outlook. A young Confederate sentry was sent to the rock for guard duty during the night. Sometime during the early morning hours, another soldier discovered him sleeping, and the commanding officer had the sentry executed for dereliction of duty.

View Raven Rock and watch for the bobbing light:

Parking/Overlook:
Combs Overlook
U.S. 23 Jenkins, Kentucky 41537 (37.157964, -82.636888)

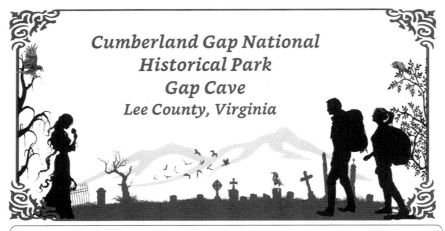

The Dead Soldier in Gap Cave

Natural chemicals in rainwater seep into the earth and eat away at the limestone over thousands of years, forming a karst cave. Gap Cave is considered a karst cave, and although explorers have visited at least 18 miles of it, ranger-led hikes cover only a tiny 0.25 fraction of the cave.

Explorer Tomas Walker, who organized the first known English expedition through Cumberland in 1750 and named the Cumberland Gap, recorded many notable locations. One was a cavern near the point where Kentucky, Tennessee, and Virginia now come together. Walker called it Gap Cave. By 1819, sawmills, gristmills, and blast machinery from the Cumberland Iron Works were powered by the spring from the cave, and from its source, a small but growing settlement called Cumberland Gap was founded.

After that, workers mined saltpeter in its depths. The cave was well-known when the Civil War rolled around. Confederate and Union troops used and explored the lower part of Gap Cave, called King Solomon's Cave, and the upper named Soldier's Cave which was also utilized as a military hospital.

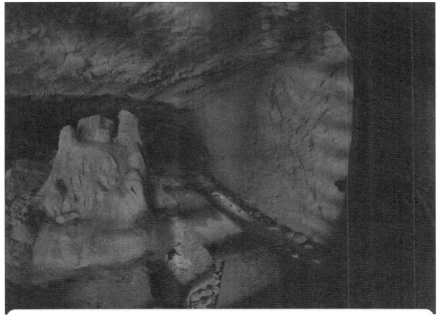

Entering the dark depths of the haunted cave—For a time, it was called Cudjo's Cave by its owner as a marketing tool for tourists, named for a fictional character in a novel who had escaped slavery and had found shelter in a similar cave.

During this time, a spirit was left behind when troops departed. For years after the war, those visiting the tunnel have observed a heavy-set man wearing a Confederate officer's jacket, pants, and boots. He has a long, gray beard that wavers at his belly, and his eyes are hollow like the corpse of a dead man long-rotted.

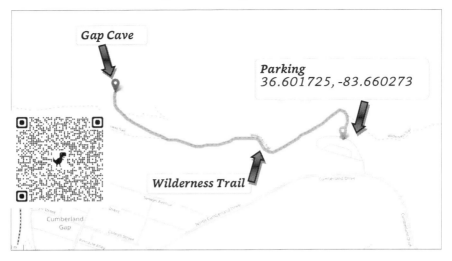

Hike to Gap Cave and try to find the ghostly officer:

Parking/Trailhead:
Daniel Boone Visitor Center Along
Old Wilderness Trail
168 N Cumberland Road
Ewing, Virginia 24248 (36.601725, -83.660273)

Hike: 0.5 miles, one-way. Out and back. Along Old Wilderness Trail. Gap Cave (36.602814, -83.667005)
Ranger-led Tour: A 1.5-mile tour of the cave interior is moderately strenuous, including the mile hike along the historic Wilderness Road. There is a fee for the excursion.

The path to Gap Cave is a part of the old Wilderness Road, a trail through Kentucky by way of Cumberland Gap that westward-bound settlers in the 1700s took and was forged by Daniel Boone. Perhaps along the trail, hikers will encounter a ghost or two of pioneers who journeyed through.

Kentucky

Pine Mountain State Resort Park
Clear Creek Hollow Trail
Bell County, Kentucky

Ghost at Clear Creek Hollow

Along this old railroad bed tucked into beautiful Clear Creek Hollow, there is a spirit from a time before workers laid the tracks, and when it was little more than a buffalo trace that explorers used as a path.

There is an abandoned Louisville and Nashville Railroad spur in an isolated hollow at the base of Pine Mountain. It once serviced the Appalachian coal mining operations and followed the path of a stream called Clear Creek. But even before the railway came through these once-remote areas, old traces or paths used by buffalo, Native Americans, and explorers like Daniel Boone followed the route of Clear Creek, once known as Buffalo Creek.

The trail and old rail tunnel where a ghost is seen—

Along the old track, there is a tunnel cut through the stone of the hillside, along with trestles crossing the creek. At the tunnel, hikers have come across remnants of the trace's past—a ghostly early 1800s frontiersman appears, then vanishes in the thickly wooded area.

The old rail tunnel—

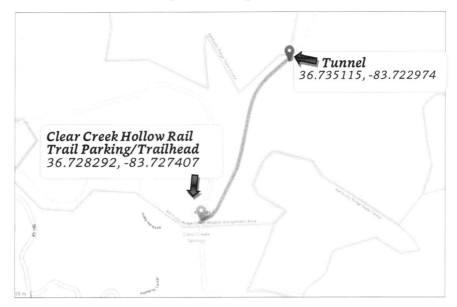

Hike Clear Creek Fitness Trail and watch for the ghostly frontiersman:

Parking/Trailhead:
Clear Creek Fitness Trail
State Hwy 1491
Pineville, Kentucky 40977
(36.728292, -83.727407)

Hike: 0.5 miles to the tunnel, one-way. Out and back. A flat, graveled path follows Clear Creek Fitness Trail, a converted railway bed. There is a sign partway stating that the park maintenance ends at this point, and after, it is private property beyond. Continue onward, but stay on the old rail bed as it is private property on either side of the trail.

Hikers cross two trestle bridges to the tunnel along a heavily wooded and scenic area, paralleling the rolling Clear Creek. **Tunnel**: (36.735115, -83.722974) Hikers can also continue 1.2 miles (for 1.3 miles, one-way) to the trail's end. Along the way, watch for the historic lumber mill on the far side of the creek and the structures to divert water for power to run the mill's machinery.

Pine Mountain State Resort Park
Chained Rock Trail
Bell County, Kentucky

Chained Rock

Chained Rock on Pine Mountain—making folks feel safe in the town below—

A huge rock has always ominously loomed over a community called Pineville along the Wilderness Road, appearing ready to tumble down the mountainside, crushing the homes in the narrow valley below. Children, troubled by the thought of those boulders releasing from Pine Mountain, were consoled by their mamas and daddies that they would never fall; they were chained to the walls.

Then people from outlying areas, upon hearing the story, traveled to Pineville to find the legendary chained rock. They were sorely disappointed to find there was none.

In 1933, it was decided, amongst a few in the community, to place a chain on the huge rock. So they dubbed themselves *The Chained Rock Club*. With the help of CCC, the Kiwanians, the Boy Scouts, and a four-mule team on June 24, 1933, they dragged a huge chain, nearly 3000 pounds from an old quarry steam shovel, to the top of the mountain and across an abyss. Then they anchored the chain with 24-inch bolts. And it still protects the town today and can be visited by a trail at Chained Rock, Pine Mountain State Park.

Trail—

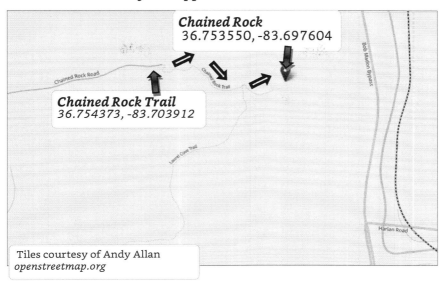

Hike to the legendary Chained Rock:

Parking/Trailhead:
Chained Rock Trailhead
Chained Rock Lookout Road
Pineville, Kentucky 40977
(36.754373, -83.703912)

Hike: Chained Rock: 0.5 miles, one-way. Out and back. Trail winds through woods to Chained Rock, lots of wooden and stone steps—mildly strenuous. There is a point toward the top where steps are carved into a stone incline to get to the rock that may make be uncomfortable for persons afraid of heights. However, it is a short journey. Downhill on the way in, uphill on the way out.

Chained Rock: (36.753550, -83.697604)

The Phantom Light of Sloans Valley Tunnel

There is a tunnel hidden in Kentucky. It has a ghost story attached to it. I found out the rail trail was abandoned due to the high cost of maintaining it safely. There is hope that it will be opened again. But until then, if you are driving near Sloans Valley along Highway 27 near Dixie Bend Road, open your window and listen. You may hear the sounds of the dead rising from the tunnel below!

On the western boundaries of the Daniel Boone National Forest, there is a little hamlet called Sloans Valley. At one time, many Cincinnati Southern Railway trains rumbled past the community and through a tunnel that held the town's name. The tunnel was the site of a horrible train wreck in the late 1800s, and from it came ghosts.

In the early hours of October 22, 1890, two trains running along The Cincinnati Southern Railway collided in Elihu, Kentucky. During the cleanup, two passenger trains were held in Somerset, approximately six miles away, and a northbound freight train was sidetracked at Sloans Valley. When the track cleared, the passenger trains continued along the line. The first train passed the freight train, but the engineer forgot about the second passenger train and pulled out. Less than a quarter mile away and within Sloans Valley Tunnel, the two met head-on. A blaze of fire followed the explosion of the cars. By luck, the passenger train had yet to enter the tunnel. Those within were able to escape through three sleeper cars that had not overturned. However, seven in the front of the train were not so fortunate and died, most of them railroad men, including Engineer John Pimlott, Fireman Welsh and Fireman Gould, Brakeman John Montgomery, and Postal Clerk Doegen.

The screams of those unable to flee filled the tunnel to the horror of onlookers who had rushed to the scene. A messenger for the U.S. Express named Ed Rufner was unharmed in the crash but could not get through the mangled bits of the smashed cars. A rescuer braved the flames with an ax, trying desperately to cut a hole through the metal, but could not get through in time. Rufner was said to have called out to the man to save himself, as it was too late for him. It was reported that amidst his blood-curdling cries, he tore at his hair and clothes as they caught afire before his charred trunk fell to the ashes and succumbed to the flames. After, those who took the tracks would often see a light bobbing up and down, working its way from one end to the other. It appeared like a lit lantern, and whoever carried it was rushing through at a dead run as if trying to warn those entering to stay away. When approached, the lantern vanished, and moans followed.

The Old Haunted Cave

About 70 years after a failed tuberculosis sanatorium closed inside a cave, tourists visit the old huts used for the patients. They can still be visited today and there are ghosts there—Image circa 1912: Library of Congress.

In 1839, Louisville Doctor John Croghan purchased a former saltpeter mine and cave tourist attraction called Mammoth Cave, along with the slaves from its estate.

Among these enslaved people was an African American explorer named Stephen Bishop, who not only acted as a tour guide in the cave but also studied the deep recesses of the cave, making enormous discoveries and providing an intricate early mapping system. In the early 1840s, the doctor also constructed two stone cabins and eight wooden huts within the cave. Speculating that the air within the cave had curative properties, he came up with a venture offering wealthy patients with tuberculosis, an infectious disease targeting the lungs, a possible breathing treatment. The cause of the disease, at the time, was unknown, and there was no cure yet. The buildings became a sanatorium, and 15 to 20 patients from 1842 to 1843 paid the doctor a large sum for the benefits. Croghan's infirmary project failed—the patients within only seemed to grow weaker, hindered by the oil lanterns and fires burning within the cave to light the dark interior, the muggy air, and the bleak and dismal atmosphere.

In 1859, travel writer Bayard Taylor took a trip to Mammoth Cave and was led past these buildings by the legendary early guides Stephen Bishop and Alfred Croghan, and he wrote this:

We passed several stone and frame houses, some of which were partly in ruin. The guide pointed them out as the residence of a number of consumptive patients who came in here in September, 1843, and remained until January. "I was one of the waiters who attended upon them," said Alfred. "I used to stand on that rock and blow the horn to call them to dinner. There were fifteen of them, and they looked more like a company of skeletons than anything else." One of the number died here. His case was hopeless when he entered, and even when conscious that his end was near he refused to leave. I can conceive of one man being benefited by a residence in the cave, but the idea of a company of lank, cadaverous invalids wandering about in the awful gloom and silence, broken only by their hollow coughs— doubly hollow and sepulchral there—is terrible.

Actually, his patients worsened. Five died within the cave, and the doctor laid their bodies out on a slab of stone, known as Corpse Rock, before returning to their families for burial or burial in the Guide Cemetery above the cave. Doctor Croghan closed his infirmary and took the remaining living patients above ground. There are whispers that the souls of some of the patients remain below ground where they once took refuge. When it is quiet, guided guests hear gentle coughing and hacking of the dead.

A drawing of Stephen Bishop holding a candle, taking a tour group through Mammoth Cave. Image NPS.org

But the cave had guides long before Croghan attempted to cure tuberculosis. The first known tour was around 1816 into the cave. Traditions passed down from local families divulge the cave was discovered in the late 1700s by John Houchin, who was hunting bears when one began to chase him. While in pursuit, he found shelter within the cave.

Many legends have stemmed from its early years of mining and then the days of the first owner Franklin Gorin utilizing enslaved people as cave guides after making the homestead of an earlier caretaker into a guesthouse.

When owners found the cave profitable for tourism, rumors thrived that there were two entrances. However, the second entrance was not on the same properties, so any monies taken in by visitors would be dispersed between the two estates. At the time, there was a slave guide who was well-versed in the many tunnel systems of the cave. The man who owned Mammoth Cave told him that he would award his freedom if he showed him the second entrance. The guide agreed, and on the day that he was to prove the existence of the alleged second entrance, the owner and a second man stayed at the entry on the premise so that the guide did not mislead them and return the same way. However, after most of the day had passed, the guide exited the second entrance, then hiked back to the primary entrance as proof. Then sometime during the night, the second entrance was secretly altered so that it no longer existed. Still today, no one knows its location.

Old Guide Cemetery—Image NPS.org

The guide earned his freedom, although he continued conducting tours at the cave. After some years, he passed away, and his family buried him in a cemetery near the cave. When a new owner took over the business, he thought it would be a grand idea to dig up the guide's body, rebury it near the cave's entrance, and place a monument nearby for tourists to gaze upon.

Then sometime during the early 1890s, a tour finished near the mouth of the cave. Those in the party decided to linger there before returning to the guesthouse. As the night filled the sky, a man in a white shirt and dark pants appeared before them. At first thought, they believed the guide had returned, and one man stepped forward to question him, and the figure vanished!

The next night after a discussion of the peculiar event, the curious decided to go back to the cave and see if the ghost appeared again. Sure enough, the shadowy man floated past them after a short time while they situated themselves in different positions. One man raised a gun and shot at the form, only to watch it vanish. As they proceeded forward, the figure appeared again, and as the men rushed toward it, it faded away. Over time and as the story of the spirit spread, more people flooded to the cave to see it at the entrance until, at a certain point, the owner reburied the guide's old bones back in the cemetery.

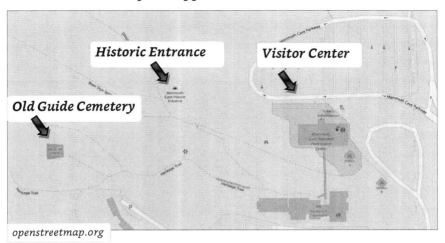
openstreetmap.org

Hike the trails of Mammoth Cave, and search for ghosts of long-gone explorers and guests:

Parking/Trailhead:
Mammoth Cave National Park
Visitor Center parking lot
Mammoth Cave, Kentucky 42259
(37.188096, -86.100628)
Violet City Lantern Tour—3.0 miles.
(There is a charge)

Old Guide Cemetery:

Trailhead/Small Parking Area: (37.186179, -86.104273)
Hike: 0.3 miles from Visitor Center. The path is along the Heritage Trail in front of the Mammoth Cave Hotel.
Cemetery: (37.186641, -86.104917)

Historic Entrance to Mammoth Cave:

Trailhead: (37.18754, -86.10355)
Hike: 0.2 miles from Mammoth Cave Park Visitor Center. The Dixon Cave Trail is 0.7 miles. Out and back. Trails lead to the collapse of the Dixon Cave entrance and the Historic Entrance at the park. A path runs down a series of steps; at the junction, take a left-hand turn on the trail.
Dixon Cave: (37.189798, -86.105490)

Kentucky State Parks
Blue Licks Battlefield Resort Park
Robertson County, Kentucky
Nicholson County, Kentucky

They Rise from the Battlefield

Kentuckians, including Daniel Boone, fight at Blue Licks—

On August 19, 1782, settlers, including Daniel Boone, living near present-day Mt. Olivet, Kentucky, set off in pursuit of British, Canadian, Shawnee, and Wyandots who had attempted to attack their fort. When they got close on a rise at what is now Blue Licks State Park, they attacked rather recklessly finding themselves fired upon from above.

Realizing they were at a disadvantage and panicking, the men began to retreat, and the enemy chased them down the hillside where the Licking River made a u-shape of the valley. Only by crossing the river were some able to escape death. But not all. Between the two battling parties, 79 were killed, including Daniel Boone's 23-year-old son, Israel. Between the two parties, 79 died during the battle.

You can walk around the park, see where the battle played out and hike the eerie trail settlers took to escape. You might see something from the past arise from the grave as hikers have seen ghostly fighters from the battle appear, then vanish. Others witness apparitions of early settlers going about their daily tasks. Some walk the hillside leading to the river and linger near the cemetery.

Licking River Trail—

Hiking to the mass burial site—

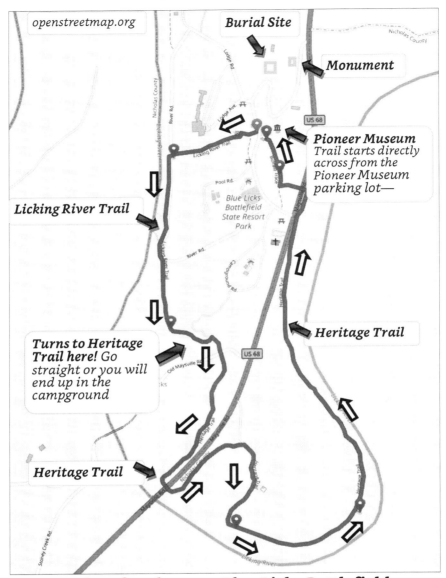

Explore for ghosts at Blue Licks Battlefield:
Parking/Trailhead:
Blue Licks Battlefield State Resort Park-Pioneer Museum
Maysville Road
Carlisle, Kentucky 40311 (38.431982, -83.993116)

Hike: Licking River Heritage Trail: 3.1 miles. Loop. Some slightly steep climbs. Across the park road from the Pioneer Museum parking lot, follow the Licking River Trail until it turns into Heritage Trail. No dogs.

Middle Creek National Battlefield
Floyd County, Kentucky

Unease

The Middle Creek Battlefield, where neighbor fought neighbor and brother fought brother. And ghostly remnants of this past still linger.

The Big Sandy Valley stretches through mountains along the Kentucky and West Virginia border through nine counties. It is rugged and so much so that it was considered low in military priority in the early part of the Civil War.

Those living within its corridor were divided on which side they chose, pitting neighbors and family members against each other. It was not uncommon for one son to leave to fight for the North and the other to fight for the South. And with a lot of recruitment administered locally, in battles, those on opposing sides quite often knew each other well.

Its strategic importance would take a front seat in 1862 to both Confederates and the Union. The Confederates needed it to block an invasion into Tennessee, and the Union needed it as a possible route into Tennessee. Both knew it would be problematic if the other had control of the valley as the Big Sandy River flowing through it was an important tributary to the Ohio River.

It is difficult today when zooming along KY-114 and through the beautiful vast valley of thickly wooded forest blended with family farms around Prestonsburg that there was ever an intense and bloody battle here, brother against brother, neighbor against neighbor. But on January 10, 1862, the Union soldiers, under the command of a relatively unknown Colonel, James A. Garfield, later a president of the U.S., attacked Confederates under the charge of Brig. Gen. Humphrey Marshall and his Confederate soldiers at Middle Creek. The Union forces fought up the ridges, and the Confederates fought their way downward. It resulted in the collapse of Confederate control in Eastern Kentucky and was the largest Civil War battle in the state.

Although relatively few men died (figures range from 15 to 27 men), strange things happen on the battlefield today. Occasionally, those walking the trail have experienced what they describe as "an eerie unease," and hear the ghostly sound of men fighting, but the source of the noise cannot be found.

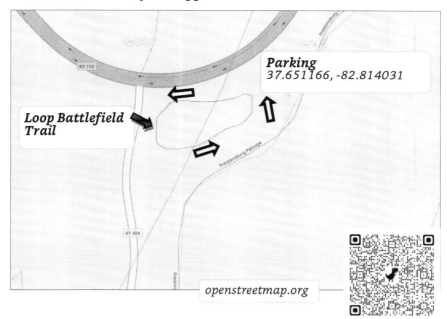

Hike the trail at the Middle Creek Battlefield and listen for ghostly remnants of its past.

Parking/Trailhead:
Middle Creek National Battlefield
2968 KY-114, Prestonsburg, Kentucky 41653
(37.651166, -82.814031)

Hike: 0.2 miles. Loop. Easy. Paved trail. Interpretive markers about battle are along the route. The battlefield also extends into a grassy field with markers.

Maryland

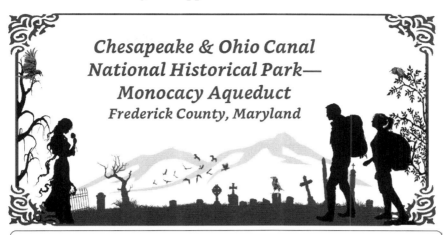

Chesapeake & Ohio Canal National Historical Park— Monocacy Aqueduct
Frederick County, Maryland

Old Raider's Treasure

Canal boat on the Monocacy Aqueduct long ago, where a ghostly lantern is witnessed bobbing across the towpath. Image:NPS.org

The Chesapeake and Ohio Canal (C&O Canal), built between 1828 and 1850 and running along the Potomac River, operated for almost a 100 years as a transportation route between Georgetown, DC to Cumberland, Maryland. It was 184.5 miles in length and had 74 canal locks, 11 aqueducts for crossing waterways, 240 culverts, tunnels, lock houses, and weirs.

It was the link to the outside market world for many remote communities. It allowed locals to float coal, lumber, and farm products along the flowing waterway and acted as a transportation route for goods, travelers, and mail. The canal was engineered to have a 2-miles-per-hour current to help the mules, led by a driver who was often a young boy or girl, walking a parallel dirt or stone towpath.

One of the obstacles when building the canal was that canal boats needed to cross natural streams along its path that were too wide for a culvert to contain. So water bridges, called aqueducts, were built to carry the boats over these large creeks and rivers that flowed into the Potomac. Canal workers erected eleven; the largest was the quartz sandstone Monocacy Aqueduct in Frederick, Maryland, which crossed the bulky Monocacy River.

John Mosby was a Confederate colonel during the Civil War who led a band of riders to conduct guerrilla warfare in northern Virginia from 1862 to 1865. He allowed his men, most between the ages of 17 to 25, to keep the loot from raids, including gold, silver, and heirlooms from private citizens; he felt it made the men happier about the war they waged. One of these raids was at Duffield's Station near Harpers Ferry. His rangers entered a car, murdered the Federal officer, and confiscated all the personal valuables of the passengers. After forcing the travelers from the train, Mosby burned the cars, but not before stealing the paymaster's box of $173,000, dividing it amongst his men.

Mosby died in 1916. Upon his deathbed, he told of treasures his guerillas buried along the countryside of Virginia because they had too much to carry from one raid to the next. Those soldiers killed in battle could not return for their spoils; if they did not tell anyone where they buried their stolen treasures, the loot still lay hidden untouched.

For years, locals passed down a story of a ghostly figure carrying a lantern on moonless nights and crossing the Monocacy Aqueduct. It was generally believed that it was the ghost of one of the thieving military men, and if the spirit was followed, it would lead to the treasure.

The Monocacy Aqueduct nowadays can be hiked—

The Chesapeake and Ohio Canal National Historical Park now maintains the canalway with a trail following the towpath. Hikers/bikers can walk/bike the towpath from Monocacy Aqueduct 18.7 miles to where the Winchester and Potomac Railroad Bridge/Appalachian Trail footbridge crosses over to Harpers Ferry. And hikers can go beyond, as the total mileage for the trail is 184.5.

In spite of the length, this particular hike will lead from the Monocacy Aqueduct to Noland's Ferry. The Noland family operated a ferry from about 1735 to 1785 that connected Carolina Road, which crossed the Potomac less than three miles from Monocacy Aqueduct. At Noland's Ferry, there was a bustling community including a store, taverns, shoemaker, tailor, wagon, and blacksmith shops. It was a connecting route for settlers, but not a safe one.

Carolina Road was nicknamed Rogues Road for all the thieves who robbed unwary travelers, drovers, and farmers coming to the market near Noland's Ferry. Some of the old canal boaters believed the ghostly lantern belonged to a robber from Noland's Ferry who buried his treasure before he was caught and jailed and who died in prison. Such either coming or going the ghostly soldier or robber will appear with his lantern and guide you to his treasure!

There is a legend of one bandit called Captain Harper who robbed and terrorized many along the road so often that neither man nor woman would go the route by night. Yet, one dark evening a fair young woman walking home from a visit with a neighbor watched as a rider slowed beside her. He asked why she was out on the road alone and, "Are you not afraid you will be accosted by the infamous Captain Harper and his band?"

"No," she replied with a shrug of her shoulders. "I have heard that Captain Harper is a gentleman." The horseman stared down at her long and hard, then dismounted and walked her safely to the gate of her home. Before leaving on his way, he bowed and tipped his hat. "Captain Harper bids you good night."

Haunted Hikes of the Appalachian Hills & Hollers 2

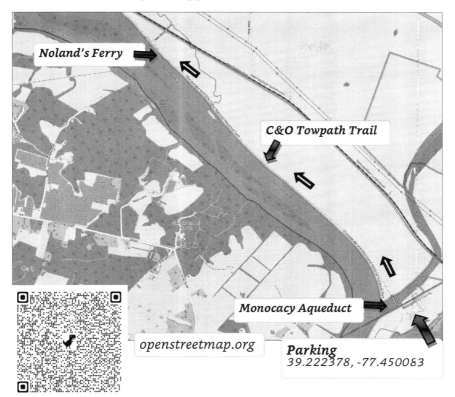

Watch for the ghosts of early raiders along the C&O Towpath Trail and search for their treasure:

Parking/Trailhead:
Mouth of Monocacy Road
Dickerson, Maryland 20842
(39.222378, -77.450083)

Hike: 0.2 miles, one-way. Out and back. Hikers can take the trail across Monocacy Aqueduct and return.

Longer Hike: 2.7 miles, one-way. Out and back. Hikers can continue to Noland's Ferry for a longer path.
Nolands Ferry C&O Canal
Tuscarora, MD 21790
(39.249516, -77.482286)

Chesapeake & Ohio Canal National Historical Park— Paw Paw Tunnel
Allegany County, Maryland

Headless Haunt

Paw Paw Tunnel in early years with a canal boat coming through—

It took nearly 6 million bricks to build the 3,118-foot Paw Paw Tunnel in the 1830s and almost bankrupted the Chesapeake and Ohio Canal Company. The Chesapeake and Ohio Canal Project built the tunnel to bypass difficult terrain along the Potomac River including river bends. Most of the laborers (about 44 were employed to work at a time) were Irish or German immigrants who spent 12-15 hours a day in backbreaking work, cutting their way through mountains and steep rock walls with black-powder blasts.

Others stood in knee-deep water with shovels and picks, digging the trench where the boats would travel. The canal workers had strikes and riots and fought amongst themselves. Violence, due to prejudice between the English, Dutch, Irish and German workers, flared up often. The workers' homes were shanties in makeshift camps that barely kept the summer heat and chilly winter winds away. The company paid laborers very little to put more money in the pockets of the investors and offered no medical care. The drinking water was often contaminated, leading to outbreaks of cholera. Typhoid fever, dysentery, malaria, and yellow fever would spread through a camp, death picking and choosing amongst those within who would be buried in mass graves or alone with a simple wood or stone marker, now long gone. Records of deaths are scarce; no one will ever know how many canal laborers and family members died along its path and near Paw Paw Tunnel.

Paw Paw Tunnel nowadays—

Upon completion, it was so narrow that it could only fit one boat at a time; there were stories of boat captains refusing to allow the right of way. So determined to go first when met with another boat coming in a different direction, stalemates would occur halfway through. One standoff between two captains lasted three days, and others waiting in a long line of boats to pass through Paw Paw Tunnel finally burned logs at one end to smoke them out.

Within Paw Paw Tunnel where ghosts have been seen—

The Paw Paw Tunnel was used as part of the canal through 1924 and is now a part of the Chesapeake & Ohio Canal National Historical Park. For years, local legends told of a headless man who haunted the tunnel. People walking the dark interior have seen shadows lurking when nobody else is around and have heard voices conversing with heavy accents like the early immigrants who lived, worked, and died there.

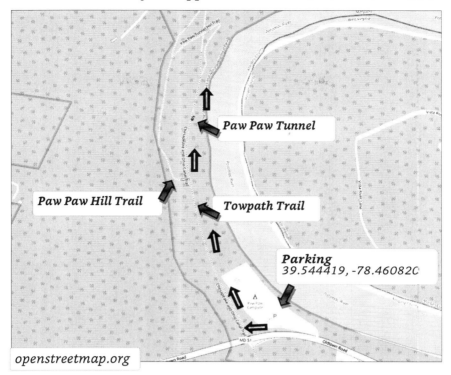

Hike to Paw Paw Tunnel and watch out for the headless man:

Parking/Trailhead:
Chesapeake and Ohio Canal Towpath
Off Oldtown Road SE (MD-51)
Oldtown, Maryland 21555
(39.544419, -78.460820)

Hike: 0.5 miles, one-way. Out and back. It is a level hike or bike ride from the parking area to the tunnel.

Longer Hike: 1.2 miles. Loop. Hikers can continue along the canal towpath trail. For a more strenuous trek, hikers can take the Paw Paw Tunnel *Hill* Trail (at about 0.3 miles along the towpath trail on the left and before the tunnel), which goes over the mountain and to the upstream tunnel entrance, then go through the tunnel and head back to the parking area.

Green Ridge State Forest— Stickpile Tunnel
Allegany County, Maryland

Stickpile

The rugged path to Stickpile Tunnel—

In the 1800s, timbermen heavily logged the land that is now much of Green Ridge Forest for the abundant wood. When little was left but stumps and scrubby brush, the Mertens family purchased 32,000 acres, cleared and burned whatever remained, and developed it into a huge apple orchard from 1870 to 1920.

CULTIVATING NEWLY-PLANTED APPLE ORCHARDS, GREEN RIDGE VALLEY, MARYLAND

A worker cultivates the area near Stickpile Tunnel, once Mertens' growing apple orchard, but now Green Ridge State Forest—

In the early years, a tiny village called Green Ridge Station, was made up of mostly lockkeepers for the Chesapeake and Ohio Canal. Those living there had little contact with the outside world until the Western Maryland Railroad paved a path through the area along with bridges and tunnels. The town grew, and the railway also offered the Mertens a way to sell apples to outside buyers. Later the orchard was sold as lots to those who wished to invest in the apple industry. In no time, the town boasted a bunkhouse for workers, a jelly factory, a store, a post office, a railroad office, a warehouse, and packing shed, and the Mertens Saloon. The Mertens orchard business went bankrupt in 1917, the land was eventually abandoned, and the forest crept into what was once a thriving town. Those who remained left their homes for better jobs or found work with the canal or railroad. In the 1970s, workers removed the railroad tracks leaving little more than an abandoned tunnel and an old railway path.

The remains of the Mertens Orchard Headquarters at Green Ridge—directly across from the gravel pull-off where I parked.

Sometime over the early years, when train wheels grinded along the tracks and its shrill whistle cried out on this lonely route, the 1,705 feet long Green Ridge Tunnel became known as Stickpile Tunnel. As the story goes, a hobo was killed inside the tunnel, and his body was carelessly covered with sticks. Since that time, those traveling through or near the tunnel have seen the hobo's ghost within.

The interior of Stickpile Tunnel where a ghost has been seen. While I was videotaping, I could hear the haunting cooing echo of pigeons that were roosting inside. Then a ghostly voice swept up among the pigeon chatter that sounded like someone calling, "Sonny!"

The Roby Cemetery—(39.5928242, -78.4294)
Just a 0.5 short hike up the gravel Carroll Road.

The entrance is gated to protect hibernating bats—and as I found out, roosting pigeons making eerie, warning coos as I walked up to the tunnel.

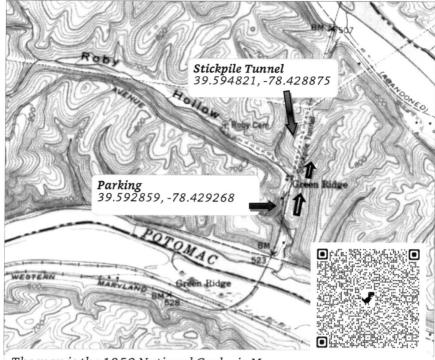

The map is the 1950 National Geologic Map Database project (NGMDB), which still showed Stickpile Tunnel, locations of buildings, and the Roby Cemetery. The trail to the tunnel is short, but for the adventurous who like old, long-gone ghost towns, there are graveled/dirt roadways to hike.

Peer into Stickpile Tunnel and wait for a ghostly hobo to appear:

Parking/Trailhead: (39.592859, -78.429268) The roadway to the site is graveled but is better suited for trucks/jeeps/or cars with four-wheel drive.

Hike: 0.07 miles, one-way. Out and back. The walk is short and mucky (the old rail path is easily visible at the pull-off), and hikers cannot enter the tunnel as a gate bars the opening to protect the bats inside. However, you can peer into the shadowy depths of the tunnel and, perhaps, see the ghost.

There are many old roads to hike and explore the old ghost town and its cemetery.

Chesapeake & Ohio Canal National Historical Park— Great Falls—Goldmine Trail (Great Falls Tavern Area)
Montgomery County, Maryland
Fairfax County, Virginia

Goldmine Ghoul

The ruins of a goldmine along the Goldmine Trail at Chesapeake & Ohio Canal National Historical Park. A ghost has long been known to walk here—

In the autumn of 1861, as the United States found itself at the beginning of a civil war, the 71st Pennsylvania Volunteer Infantry Regiment was encamped near the Potomac River and Great Falls to guard against Confederate attacks across the Potomac after the first Battle of Bull Run.

Image depicting the discovery of gold by a soldier at Great Falls while washing dishes — U.S. National Park Service

There was a soldier named McCleary among them who had been at the California gold fields, and legends passed down reveal that he saw tiny flecks of gold in the bottom of the cooking pots when he was using the sand from a nearby creek to scour them clean at Great Falls. McCleary paused to collect some stones into a cotton sack on Spring Creek one day and was approached by the owner of the land, Dick Collins, as he was on his way home from plowing a field. McCleary asked if he could break up some of the stones, and Collins approved his request saying, "We might need all the rocks you can pile up if the rebels ever cross the Potomac."

We may never know if McCleary divulged the truth to Collins and that he had found gold there. However, he quietly pledged to himself that he would return one day after the war and buy the land to extract the gold. After his discharge, he returned to the area, organized a group of backers, purchased the Collins farm where he discovered the gold, and formed the Maryland Mining Company. Although workers sunk a shaft in 1867, miners never found enough gold to make it rich, abandoning their work two years later.

The mine passed through several hands throughout the years, but when it was still in use during the early 1900s, the company added a second shaft hoping to cut deeper into a more valuable vein. While digging this shaft on June 15, 1906, the miners lingered at the hoist house, enjoying a drink and a chat before going underground for work. One of the men snatched up a bottle, and another had a box of dynamite that he rested on a bench in the building.

At that time, miners wore headgear for a light source that consisted of a canvas hat with a brim and a metal oilwick cap lamp near the forehead to provide illumination enough to see directly in front of their faces. Smokey and leaving soot on their faces, the caps were both uncomfortable and reeking of oil, and miners took them off immediately after leaving the mines. At some point, one of the miners took off his cap and laid it on the bench. It ignited the fuse for the dynamite. It appeared that most heard the sizzling sound as the fuse began to burn, and they ran from the building. One did not. The explosion killed Charles Eglin, the hoist man whose job was to raise and lower loads up and down the shaft.

After the explosion at the mine, mysterious sounds issued—Image: C&O Canal National Historic Park.

Not long after the explosion, nightwatchmen began to complain about hearing the mysterious sound of footsteps crunching on the gravel paths near the mine office and other buildings; however, they could find no source of the sounds. Others working in the offices would hear knuckles knocking on the doors. When they opened the doors, nobody was there. An old tame mare pulled the wagons for the company. She did so up until the event without even a click of the tongue to prod her. After Eglin died, she refused to go near the gate and would rear and snort as if terrified of something no one could see.

Hikers can peer through the fence enclosure to the ruins of the mine. A blacksmith shop and outbuildings are among the tumbling buildings where a ghost would follow nightwatchmen. It was generally believed to be a tommyknocker—to some, the ghost of a dead miner, and to others, a fairy that played tricks on the workers.

Some miners swore they heard the thumping of tommyknockers within the dark depths of the mine late at night. They blamed all sorts of bad luck at the Maryland Mine on these tiny, supernatural, fairy-like creatures, from shafts filling up with water because the pumps were not turned on to workers unable to get to a vein because mine shafts were dug too short.

The Maryland Mine operated sporadically and closed for good in the 1940s. Today, the land is operated by the Chesapeake & Ohio Canal National Historical Park, Great Falls Tavern Area. Hikers can take the Gold Mine Trail and see evidence of the mine operation along with wayside exhibits, including the location the ghost and tommyknockers pestered the miners.

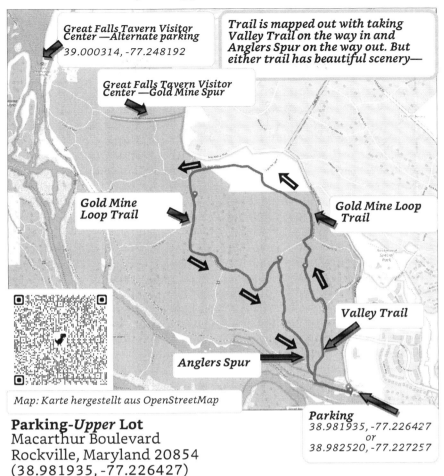

Map: Karte hergestellt aus OpenStreetMap

Parking-*Upper* Lot
Macarthur Boulevard
Rockville, Maryland 20854
(38.981935, -77.226427)

Hike: Goldmine Trail— Loop.

Hike from Upper Lot to Anglers or Valley Trail Spur/Trail to Gold Mine Trail: Out and Back.

Approximately 2.9 miles total with either spur.

From the **Upper Lot** at Great Falls Parking, take the Berma Road trailhead (38.981870, -77.226806). It is a foot-traffic-only old gravel road. Hikers follow along the road for about 0.1 miles to a large fence enclosure along the path.
Then, to the right and nearly hidden, there are trailheads (38.98262, -77.22912) of Anglers Spur (noted by white tree markers—0.5 miles) and Valley Trail (0.6). Either will take hikers to the Gold Mine Loop Trail (1.6 miles) marked by blue tree markers. Loop trail with spurs. Well-maintained. With historical signs.

Parking-*Lower* Lot
Macarthur Boulevard
Rockville, Maryland 20854
(38.982520, -77.227257)

Goldmine Trail: Loop.

Hike from Lower Lot to Anglers or Valley Trail Spurs/Trail
to get to Gold Mine Trail: Out and Back.
Approximately 2.9 miles total with either spur.
There are two trailheads if parked at the **Lower Lot** of Great Falls Parking. The trail with the gates to the right is the proper trail toward Gold Mine Trail. Hikers immediately come to a series of wooden steps that take them upward to a graveled and foot-traffic-only Berma Road.
(38.982090, -77.227701).

Hikers follow along the road for about 0.1 miles to a large fence enclosure along the path. Then, to the right and nearly hidden, there are trailheads (38.98262, -77.22912) of Anglers Spur (noted by white tree markers—0.5 miles) and Valley Trail (0.6). Either will take hikers to the Gold Mine Loop Trail (1.6 miles) marked by blue tree markers. Loop trail with spurs. Well-maintained. With historical signs.

If the parking lots are full, here is an alternative parking lot and trailhead:

Hike from Great Falls Tavern Visitor Center:
Approximately 3.2 miles with Gold Mine Spur and Goldmine Loop Trail.

Alternate Parking: Hikers should arrive early; the Upper and Lower Parking Lots fill quickly. If the lots are full, hikers can pay to enter **Great Falls Tavern Visitor Center** and take the Gold Mine Spur to Gold Mine Trail.

Great Falls Tavern Visitor Center
11710 Macarthur Boulevard
Potomac, Maryland 20854
(39.000314, -77.248192)

Haunted Hikes of the Appalachian Hills & Hollers 2

Antietam National Battlefield— Burnside's Bridge
Washington County, Maryland

Phantoms of the Deadliest Battle

The U.S. Civil War left many dead in its path. It also left many ghosts, like those at Burnside's Bridge after the Battle of Antietam. Image: NPS.org

In September of 1862, during the Civil War, the Confederate army, led by General Robert E. Lee, entered Maryland in hopes of invading north into Pennsylvania for its first strategic *offensive* action against the Union Army.

Up until that point, the Confederacy had been on the defensive. On September 17, 1862, on Antietam Creek near Sharpsburg, Maryland, the Confederate and Union armies clashed mainly in an open cornfield in the morning and then along an old sunken path, later dubbed Bloody Lane, until it shifted south. For over three hours in the afternoon, 500 Confederate soldiers held an area overlooking a bridge against great odds. They were finally forced to retreat when Union General Ambrose Burnside's soldiers pushed them back and captured the bridge.

Burnside's Bridge, back, and stone fence, front. Note the line of graves between the arrows marked by crude pieces of wood. Ghosts show themselves here. Image: NPS.org

The Battle of Antietam became the deadliest one-day battle in American military history. The bridge where the battle took place would be called "Burnside's Bridge." And the location of so much death and tragedy is haunted by this past. Visitors have seen bobbing lights and shadows in the area where many Union soldiers were killed and then buried in makeshift graves.

Burnside's Bridge nowadays. You can walk to it. When taking this photo and looking closer, two ghostly soldiers appear standing in the water.

Haunted Hikes of the Appalachian Hills & Hollers 2

Parking/Trailhead:
Parking/Trailhead: Parking for Georgian's Overlook and Burnside Bridge
Old Burnside Bridge Road
Sharpsburg, Maryland 21782
(39.449957, -77.732583)

Wheelchair Accessible Parking: (39.451578, -77.733091)

Hike:
Burnside's Bridge (Lower Bridge)
18125 Old Burnside Bridge Road
Sharpsburg, Maryland 21782
(39.450520, -77.732207)

-To Burnside's Bridge: 0.2 miles, one-way. Out and back.

-Burnsides Bridge *and* Union Advance Trail: 1.2 miles. Loop. Hikers can also take the Union Advance Trail after the bridge, which loops around and back to the bridge.

Ghost along the Waste Weir

The waste weir between Locks 28 and 29 where a ghostly woman walks and creepy tree shadows writhe over the laying water—

Excess water from storms in a canal damaged its banks and caused flooding. Walls were built along the canals with wooden planks or boards inserted in slotted gates to adjust the height of the water for flooding, repairs, or emergencies. The planks in the wall were removed/added by a lock keeper to keep the water level constant. The weirs were originally made of concrete with boards atop for mule crossing.

There is a haunted waste weir between Lock 28 (Point of Rocks Lock) and Lock 29 (Catoctin Lock) at Lander and downstream from the CSX Catoctin Tunnel. Canal boatmen and locals traveling the path would see a ghostly woman walk across the towpath to the waste weir and follow it to the river before vanishing.

Standing next to the canal towpath and the waste weir where the ghostly woman walked and looking out upon the path she would take to the river—

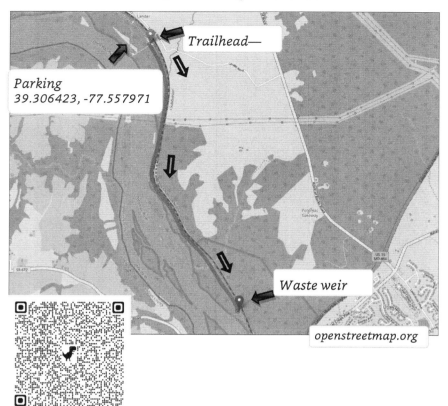

Parking/ Trailhead
Lander Boat Ramp
Jefferson, Maryland 21755
(39.306423, -77.557971)

Trailhead:
(39.306307, -77.558436)

Hike: 1.7 miles, one-way. Out and back. Flat, gravel towpath trail. Head southeast on the Chesapeake and Ohio Canal Towpath toward C&O Canal Trust Lockhouse 28 (39.281348, -77.548044), which is after the waste weir here: (39.284554, -77.550254)

Chesapeake & Ohio Canal National Historical Park— Haunted House Bend

Montgomery County, Maryland
Loudoun County, Virginia

Everlasting Swim

The Battle of Ball's Bluff left behind ghosts that scared canal boat captains and still startle hikers today—Balls Bluff left, Harrison Island, right. Image: Library of Congress

In 1861, the Union was building up the Army of the Potomac for an advance into Virginia. In October, after some clashes between Confederate and Union troops at Harpers Ferry, the Confederates appeared to be leaving Leesburg. Curious about their motives, General George McClellan, commander of United States armies in the Washington area, sent an urgent telegram to troops nearby.

He wanted them to keep an eye out on the Confederates there. Leesburg was a sought-after and strategically important position the Union wanted to capture because two of Northern Virginia's main roads crossed there. The Confederate army *had* left the area under the authority of a colonel but received orders to return immediately. And so they did.

Unbeknownst to McClellan, he ordered troops to conduct a "slight demonstration" to gauge the Confederate reaction. On the night of October 20, inexperienced scouts sent across the river to survey for Confederate camps along the steep and thickly forested cliff areas around and above the Potomac River mistook shadows and trees for a line of tents. They reported they had come across an unguarded camp. Early the next morning, Union troops were sent across the Potomac to attack the defenseless site but were surprised by a company of Mississippi infantry, and a skirmish began.

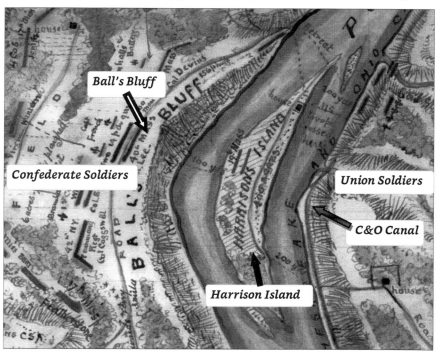

When the leader of the Union troops was killed, his soldiers panicked. They started heading back to the Potomac with the Confederates hot on their heels, driving them over a bluff and into the river where only four boats were waiting on Harrison Island nearby. Many soldiers were taken prisoner, and others were shot in the back while they frantically tried to swim across the Potomac. Still, others who could not swim drowned.

During the Battle of Ball's Bluff, the plantation house and barn on Harrison Island (not accessible and on private property) were used as hospitals which may have contributed to the bend in the river called "Haunted House Bend." Image: Maryland Historical Trust Maryland Inventory of Historic Properties Form

Harrison Island, a private island owned by the Harrison Island Conservation Society, is on a broad bend in the Potomac River between the steep slopes of Ball's Bluff to the west and the canal and towpath to the east in Maryland. The Union army utilized the island to attack Ball's Bluff. They also used the 2-story plantation house and barns on Harrison Island as temporary field hospitals during the Battle of Ball's Bluff, which most likely contributed to the famous name, *Haunted House Bend*.

Some of the dead Union soldiers were buried in its earth along with amputated limbs from the hospital, which are believed to remain there. After the battle, boatmen strictly avoided overnight stops at this section of the canal paralleling Harrison Island and across from Ball's Bluff, for dead soldiers haunted it. They were known to pester the mules, spooking the poor beasts so they refused to nibble their grains or untie them while they rested. The ghosts would also untie lines, allowing the boats to drift downstream. Captains would tie off a mile away if a canal boat did not make it to the bend by nightfall instead of venturing through after dusk.

Canal legend stated that below Mile Posts 33 and 34, ghosts from the Battle of Ball's Bluff haunted this bend. I suggest going in early spring or autumn when you can see the river and the island through bare trees—and beyond to the other side of the river to immerse yourself in the history.

Haunted Hikes of the Appalachian Hills & Hollers 2

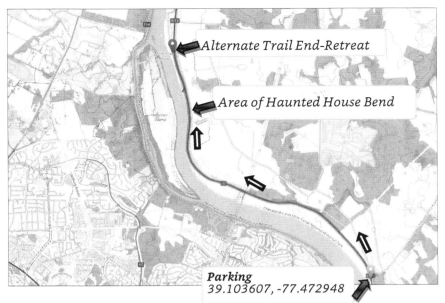

Parking/ Trailhead:
At Lock 25 (Edwards Ferry named for the Ferry operating there until 1836)
Edwards Ferry Road
Poolesville, Maryland 20837
Parking: (39.103607, -77.472948)

Trailhead:
(39.103706, -77.472680)

Hike: Easy, flat, and flat gravel. Travel along the Potomac River to Haunted House Bend and for an extra mile, one-way, to the end of Harrison Island, where many soldiers retreated.

1) Through Haunted House Bend—
3.5 miles, one-way. Out and back.
End: (39.135168, -77.515249)

2) Through the Entire bend— 4.5 miles, one-way. Out and back.
Includes most of the Union retreat route and to the end of Harrison Island, paralleling the canal towpath trail.
End: (39.149157, -77.517999)

Lockhouse 25 and Edwards Ferry—Starting point. Parking is located at the far left of the image. The path is central. To travel this route, hikers will take the towpath trail to the right of this image and past the lockkeeper's house (which can be rented!)

Haunted House Bend— I rode this one on my bike, then parked and walked. As I had heard the dead soldiers once untied mules here, I wondered if they would unlock my bike chain once I was out of sight. Perhaps they did not know my lock code, as nothing appeared touched when I returned.

West Virginia

The Red-headed Man of Dorsey's Knob

Dorsey's Knob in earlier years. The knob was named for George Dorsey of Maryland, who purchased the land in 1803, years after the fiery destruction of the Cobun (Coburn) fort nearby in 1778. Image: West Virginia and Regional History Collection, West Virginia University Libraries

In the mid-1700s, Native Americans and settlers fought over the land where Morgantown stands today. As a result, pioneers built several forts to protect themselves from constant attacks. One was Fort Cobun (Coburn), a small stockade fort established by the Johnathan Cobun (Coburn) family, who owned a parcel of land near Dorsey's Knob, a mountain summit with a rocky knob that overlooks the Monongahela River and the Appalachian Mountains.

Attacks in the region had increased in the late 1770s after government-sanctioned militia under John Murray, 4th Earl of Dunmore, had murdered Native American families in the area. However, nearby the fort and across a close creek, there were still Native Americans inhabiting the land. And they were quite resentful of the settlers' trespassing on the territory and the killing of their families.

Dorsey's Knob has been a popular tourist attraction since the 19th century. And legends arose of a ghost during this time. Image: West Virginia and Regional History Collection, West Virginia University Libraries

In the early spring of 1778, settlers, with an armed escort, were returning from planting corn about a mile from Fort Cobun. Native Americans had secreted themselves on either side of the road in the brush, ambushed the group, and began firing. Most of the party escaped safely to the fort; however, Native Americans struck two men with gunfire. Jacob Mill was shot in the belly, overtaken, tomahawked, and scalped. John Woodfin was riding a horse and was an easy target when a ball went through his leg, breaking his thigh and trapping him beneath his dying horse. Woodfin was easily captured and dragged to the rocks atop Dorsey's Knob, a focal point where all could see. His captors fashioned two poles into an "X," drove the ends into the ground, and secured their prisoner to it.

Woodfin was scalped and flayed from the top of his head to the base of his neck. He was left there to die, slowly bleeding to death. Anyone looking from the fort below would see the horrifying view of the man's bloodied corpse and red head. He remained there for quite some time before settlers could remove his body affixed to the crossed poles.

They may have removed his body, but John Woodfin's ghost remains. Some parking in the lot or hiking to the knob have run into his phantom. He wears colonial clothing, bits of cut flesh flop lazily on his shoulders, and his veined head is blood-red. He attempts to grab the unwary by the hair; most believe he is trying to replace his missing flesh with the scalp of those he seizes.

Dorsey's Knob today is part of Dorsey's Knob Park and Disc Golf Course —

There is one way to ward off this man who has come to be known as the Red-headed Man. It is to fashion two slender sticks with string, twining them together into an X or cross and carrying it while visiting the site. Even the sight of such a device as the one the Native Americans flayed him upon frightens the spirit enough to ward him off.

Haunted Hikes of the Appalachian Hills & Hollers 2

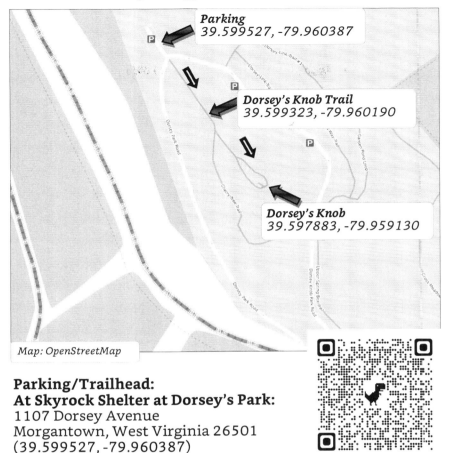

Map: OpenStreetMap

Parking/Trailhead:
At Skyrock Shelter at Dorsey's Park:
1107 Dorsey Avenue
Morgantown, West Virginia 26501
(39.599527, -79.960387)

Hike:
(39.599323, -79.960190)
0.2 miles, one-way. Out and back. Across from the parking area, hikers will see the trail leading up the short but steep climb to the summit. (39.597883, -79.959130)

Twin Falls State Park—
Hemlock Trail
Wyoming County, West Virginia

Dead Cat Settles the Score

The place of a homestead and a phantom cat along Hemlock Trail—

A stream called Dixon Branch at Twin Falls State Resort Park runs from the fringes of the campground and about a mile to Black Fork near the golf course. Those who hike the Hemlock Trail from the campground will follow its course as it parallels the winding trail. At about 0.3 miles from the campground, hikers will come across a clearing on a hillside just before the trail veers to the left into deep woodland.

Old foundation stones, washing pans, and a few other remnants are the only traces that there was once a home here. It is this home where a ghost story begins—

In the mid-1800s, a young couple built a cozy cabin on the hillside just above this section of Dixon Branch and settled in happily as newlyweds do. But when the Civil War broke out, the husband went to war. Days passed, and the wife did not hear from the man. So isolated from others in the community and feeling lonely, when a stray kitten showed up at her doorstep, she took it in, although she knew her husband despised cats. The woman easily fell deeply in love with her furry little friend. As the days turned to years without a word or a letter from her husband, the kitten grew into a cat, and the two settled in, happy with each other's company. So delighted with the one friendly feline and sure her husband had died on the battlefield, the woman took in more strays to keep her company.

But one day, a figure worked its way down the old road, then up the path to the cabin. He seemed to be a stranger, but he did not knock on the door and walked right inside. It was then the woman recognized it was her husband. She was quite disheartened because she had grown attached to her family of cats and knew he would make her get rid of them. And he forced her to do just that, except for one he allowed her to keep. However, it was not long before he began to treat the cat cruelly, kicking it away when it came near, stepping on its tail, and tossing it outside on cold winter days. The two did not get along, and the man killed the cat one day. However, before it died, the cat settled the score. It had put up a noble fight and scratched and clawed at the man's arms until they bled with deep gashes. Within a couple of weeks, the wounds on the man got infected, and he died an agonizing and slow death.

Hemlock Trail—Twin Falls State Resort Park—

After, travelers who took the old road heard the sound of a cat meowing and hissing. Nothing could be found when they searched for the source of the noises. Others would catch a glimpse of a shadowy cat in the path. When approached, it vanished.

Haunted Hikes of the Appalachian Hills & Hollers 2

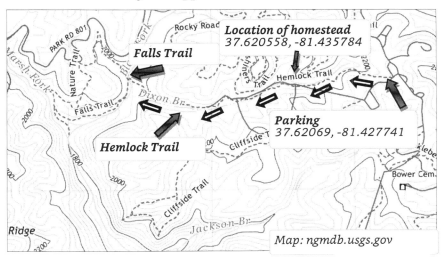

Map: ngmdb.usgs.gov

Parking/Trailhead:
Twin Falls State Resort Park Campground
Park Road 801
Mullens, West Virginia 25882
There is a one-car pull-off next to the trail located here:(37.62069, -81.427741) or ample parking in a lot with a restroom just down the park road.

Trailhead—

Hike Hemlock Trail: (Trailhead: 37.620543, -81.427638) The Hemlock Trail is 1.25 miles, one-way Out and back. Easy. The trail begins at the state park campground. It gradually descends along a path designated by blue markers. It follows a stream, Dixon Branch, and ends at the intersection of the Nature Trail and Falls Trail. The trail is well-marked, simple to follow, and exceptionally well-maintained.

Homestead—

Hike Falls Trail: Hemlock Trail ends at Falls Trail, and they connect here: (37.62, -81.449). Hikers can continue along the Hemlock Trail to **Falls Trail** (a loop trail) after crossing a wooden bridge (near the golf course) to hike the path in the next ghost story instead of driving to the Falls Trail trailhead.

Twin Falls State Park—Falls Trail
Wyoming County, West Virginia

The Headless Engineer of Cabin Creek

A lumber train in West Virginia, with engineer sitting on a log, left.
Image: West Virginia & Regional History Collection, West Virginia University

In the 1900s, between Saulsville and the Guyandotte River, there was a timbering operation with a railroad running alongside Cabin Creek. Loggers cut oak, poplar, hemlock, and chestnut on the ridges, took them by wagon and loaded them onto train cars. The train would haul the wood to the Guyandotte River, where the trunks were branded to show identification. Then, they floated free or were made into rafts by bolting and chaining logs together which headed downstream to the sawmills along its path.

Wyoming County timber on the Guyandotte River. Image: West Virginia & Regional History Collection, West Virginia University.

These loggers and rail workers had dangerous jobs. The competition was great, so bosses pushed the workers to harvest and transport the lumber at a relentless pace so the logs were processed before other companies. Then, one late afternoon and rushed by the setting sun, an engineer was speeding along the railroad bed too fast, and the wheels jumped the track. The train keeled to the side, and the engineer was killed instantly beneath the engine after it fell. When the loggers heard the explosion of cars, they rushed to the accident scene. Furiously, they sifted through the wreckage, and it was not long before they found the engineer's mashed and bloodied corpse.

But try as they might, the men could not locate his head. For many hours they searched even after dusk darkened the sky, rifling through the heavy brush along the creek. Then that night, thick, black clouds filled the sky above, and it began to storm. The bosses called off the search until the next morning.

At dawn, the men returned and still could not find the engineer's head and eventually abandoned the search so they could return to work. The water was rushing through the hollow of Cabin Creek so violently that many believed the missing head had rolled over the rocks and stones downstream during the night, and not even those with the keenest eye could recover it. Not long after the wreck, the timbermen and train operators would see a headless ghost trudging along the banks of the creek. Some dreaded working there on eves before a storm, for they knew the train engineer's ghost would appear, searching for his head.

Wyoming County— Looking at the train tracks to the left, it is easy to see why the logging trains jumped the tracks quite often! Image: West Virginia & Regional History Collection, West Virginia Univ.

Along the trail, hikers can see remnants of the old lumber railway (center)—

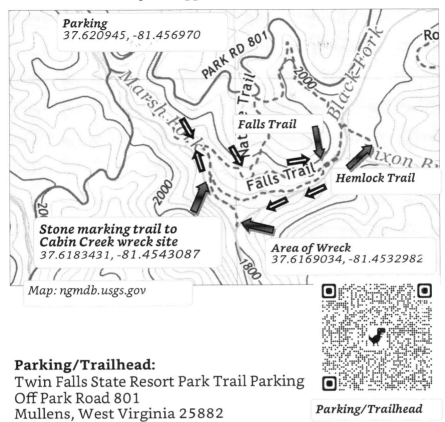

Map: ngmdb.usgs.gov

Parking/Trailhead:
Twin Falls State Resort Park Trail Parking
Off Park Road 801
Mullens, West Virginia 25882
(37.621174, -81.456959)

Hike: (Trailhead: 37.620970,-81.456803) 1.25 miles. Loop. (Not including a couple of short spurs to waterfalls if you like scrambling down steeper climbs.) Hikers can take the left trail that heads easily uphill on the way around, then downhill after it loops. The side trail leading to the wreck site is almost at the end of the loop hike and is designated by a huge stone. There are two falls. If you take the left Falls Trail, the trail is between the two waterfalls. The loop trail is very well maintained and well-marked with yellow tags and easy to follow. The side trail takes hikers through a beautiful tunnel of rhododendrons and the creek. The main Falls Trail is well-marked, simple to follow, and exceptionally well-maintained.

Falls Trail—

Stone marking the spur side trail—

Area of train derailment—and ghost.

Twin Falls State Park
Poke Hollow Trail—
Wyoming County, West Virginia

That Thing up in Poke Holler

There is something up in Poke Holler. And it is huge—

I took some trips collecting ghost stories a couple of weeks before winter set in not long ago. I stopped at Twin Falls State Resort Park for the night and decided to head off on some hiking before dark, particularly the Poke Gap Trail. A couple of years ago, when I interviewed folks about all things ghostly in the area, I got this little treat from a restaurant worker, "Well, we don't have anything I know of like that. But we've got *That Thing* up in Poke Holler. You know, the Poke Holler Monster. You like stuff like that?"

I did like stuff like that, and I told her as much. It appeared a creature outshined anything ghostly right there. And a few people had family members who had run-ins with this monster, mostly quick (but no less terrifying) sightings while hunting or driving local roads late at night.

As it goes, *That Thing* walks upright with broad shoulders and long arms and legs. It looks like a cross between a man and an ape, and it is a deep gray. Whatever it is, folks have been seeing a Bigfoot-like creature near Twin Falls State Resort Park, Saulsville, and Maben for years. It appears to come from deep in the woods around a place called Poke Hollow off Poke Hollow Road, a dark hollow within the park.

Near the town hall in Oceana, just up the road from Poke Hollow—

I found a record of this creature close by that a reporter documented in the August 1978 Independent Herald. Ten miles away in Oceana, thirty-nine-year-old patrolman Bill Pritt came face to face with a seven-foot creature right in front of the Oceana Town Hall. It was an early Monday morning—dark with fog trickling through the town tucked into the forest and mountains deep in Wyoming County.

Pritt was working with Chief Raymond Walker and was on the tail end of a twelve-hour shift—7 p.m. to 7 a.m. when dispatch received a call. A baby was screaming in a neighborhood near the Oceana Town Hall. Pritt was the closest officer to the area, and he got into his cruiser and drove to the location along Monroe Street.

"I radioed the jail and told them I'd be out of the car checking on some babies crying," Pritt disclosed not long after. "I checked this trailer, and the man said it was probably cats fighting. We couldn't find any evidence of a catfight, so we started to check the neighborhood to find out where the weird sound was coming from. It let out a squall that scared me to death. I mean, the hairs on the back of my neck stood straight up. I've never heard anything like it." Pritt was a seasoned cop; he thought he had probably seen everything. "I went on down toward Johnny Aliff's house," he went on, "and I saw what I thought was a man standing under a street light. I noticed that it was big, but he didn't move to hide from me, and with that noise, it wasn't really usual for somebody to be out there." Pritt divulged, stating it turned around with its back to him. "Then it kind of leaped, and I hollered at it. I thought it was somebody who'd been into something and was trying to get away from me, and it had jumped down over the bank to the edge of the river."

Clear Fork, where the man-like creature leaped with one step—

Pritt shined a spotlight along the Clear Fork but saw nothing. "It had jumped completely across the river. It had to have jumped because I didn't hear any splashing, and as close as I was, I would have heard if it had hit the water," Pritt stated. "I saw it moving up the bank on the other side, and I fired six shots at it. After that, I just don't remember. I was scared to death." However, it did not stop the beast from disappearing into the forest.

It was difficult for locals, DNR, and town officials to digest. They tried to call it a misplaced heron. But Pritt was adamant what he saw was no bird. "It was dark-colored, and it looked like a man. A bird has spindly legs, and a crane would have a long neck. This didn't have either. It was like a man, only big, and it must have weighed three hundred pounds. You can laugh at me and think I'm crazy if you want, but I saw it, and I don't want to see it again," the officer responded.

And there was no concern he was a credible witness; the Oceana Town Recorder was steadfast in the statement the man was a level-headed officer. Oceana Police Chief Raymond Walker, who heard Pritt's shots and made his way to the river, told reporters: "I don't think it could hurt you because it's had the opportunity to attack, and it hasn't. It's moved away, so I don't think anybody should fear for their safety." Pritt was not so convinced. "Maybe not," Pritt answered quickly, "but if I see it again, I'm sure not going to go up to it and try to start a conversation."

Most would agree with Pritt. Still, I would not mind getting a sighting of that Poke Hollow Monster. So I hiked the meandering Poke Hollow trail a couple of weeks ago, up and down, with my dog Harley. It was cold and quiet in the hollow, except for the crunch of autumn leaves beneath my boots and her sauntering paws.

Along the meandering Poke Hollow Trail—the trail is well-marked, well-maintained, and easy to follow.

The area had a mysterious aura, and I looked over my shoulder nervously more than once. Unfortunately, I did not see the monster. But it is a good excuse to go back to Twin Falls, so I think I will try again once winter comes, so maybe I can find some tracks in the snow from *That Thing* up in Poke Holler.

Map: ngmdb.usgs.gov

Parking/Trailhead:
Twin Falls State Resort Park Trail Parking
Off Park Road 803
Mullens, West Virginia 25882
(37.645607, -81.431984)

Parking/Trailhead:

Hike: 3.5 miles. Loop. Moderate with some uphill. The trail, within thick forestland, climbs to the highest point in the park. Hikers will pass two cemeteries along the route.

Tilley-Tolliver Cemetery along the trail.

Twin Falls State Park—
While You are There. . .
Bower Homestead
Park Road 801
Mullens, WV 25882
37.614427, -81.428204

Old Haunted Homestead

An old homestead at the park is haunted—

Tucked in a hollow surrounded by forest at Twin Falls is one of West Virginia's oldest still-standing cabins, circa 1835. In the 1860s, the Bower family moved into the homestead and raised a family on the farm. Above the home on a hill is the family cemetery. When the state purchased the land, the cabin was restored, and now visitors to the park can pop in and get a taste of pioneer life. They may also see a ghost or two. Visitors see spirits working along the old paths the early homesteaders once traveled. Faces peer out of the windows and full-body apparitions, mistaken for reenactors, still go about their daily chores—then vanish!

**Twin Falls State Park—
While You are There...
Picnic Area and Woods Family Cemetery**
Park Road 801
Mullens, WV 25882
37.623729, -81.427886

Playground of the Dead

Playground near the cemetery where swings move on their own—

Early settlers endured a hard life, especially in remote pockets of Appalachia. Epidemics of cholera, smallpox, typhus, yellow fever and scarlet fever wiped out entire families before vaccines were available. Just to the left of the swings, there is an old family cemetery with many children who did not make it to adulthood. Some who visit the playground and the shelter house nearby have seen the swings moving on their own as if those little spirits from a hundred years ago have come out to play with the living.

The parking area is wheelchair accessible—

New River Gorge National Park—
The Rend Trail
Fayette County, West Virginia

A Certain Likeness-Legend of McKinley Rock

McKinley Rock around 1911 with track—Image: West Virginia and Regional History Collection, West Virginia University

McKinley Rock today along trail—

The trail (3.2 miles) was originally a railway line constructed between 1901 and 1904 by Paddy Rend to his coal mines in Rend (later Minden). After the blasting of rock on a hillside to create the railroad bed on September 1, 1901, workers noticed the silhouette of President McKinley on the remaining stone cliff, which was considered an ill omen.

An ominous superstition often arose when a worker recognized the likeness of a family member after the stone wall from a rise was blasted to make way for a train or roadbed. It was always rumored that a person whose profile appeared on the rock would die. The outline of McKinley's face was said to be so horrifying to the laborers that work stopped for quite some time. Rightly so as later that day, a telegraph was relayed to the Thurmond Station that Leon F. Czolgosz had shot President McKinley in Buffalo, New York. The president would die eight days later.

The trail and three benches before the legendary McKinley Rock—

The silhouette in the stone cliff can still be viewed today. McKinley Rock tops a cliff on the Rend Trail, just before the first trestle bridge near Thurmond. It is past the bridge with the overlook and bench and just past Arbuckle Trail. To find McKinley Rock, watch for three benches on the left just before the cut in the hill. Walk a few steps past and turn your head toward the rock wall. It is easiest seen in the fall and winter.

Looking down toward Thurmond along the trail—

Take a moment and look down to the waters of the New River below. This waterway was one passageway that an early settler named Mary Draper Ingles used as a path home to Virginia after being kidnapped by Shawnee and taken to Kentucky. And there are plenty of vantage points for hikers to view the ghost town of Thurmond below (or after hiking the trail, continuing along the roadway to the town itself) on the path and perhaps see a ghost! The ghost of town founder, irregular Confederate Captain William Thurmond, would be seen riding around town on his horse after he died. He was a prohibitionist and a strict Baptist who tried earnestly to keep his community on the straight and narrow. When he first settled along the banks of the New River, there was one house and the railroad in the town, and he forbade any alcohol. Unfortunately, as the coal companies grew around him, so did a certain amount of lawlessness. In 1892, the McKell family built the Dunglen Hotel east of Thurmond's land. It was notorious for its red-light district. William Thurmond died in 1910 at the age of 90, and his spirit rode through the town, watching over it and protecting it from the drunk and rowdy.

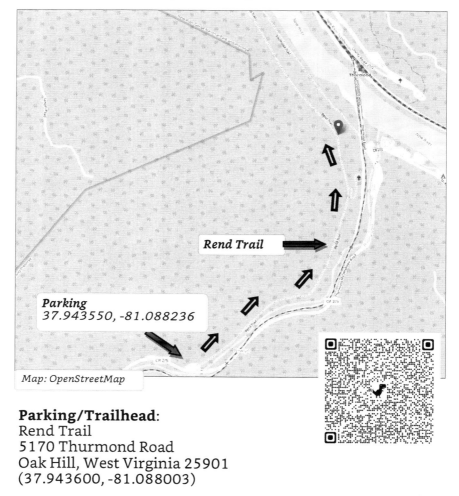

Parking/Trailhead:
Rend Trail
5170 Thurmond Road
Oak Hill, West Virginia 25901
(37.943600, -81.088003)

Hike: 1.0 miles, one-way. Hikers can continue for a total of 3.2 miles, although check for bridge closures between trailhead and Minden. There are also trails leading into Thurmond to explore the town and the Southside Trail to see the sights along the river.

Harpers Ferry—
Appalachian Trail
Virginius Island Trail
Jefferson County, West Virginia

A Haunted Hike Through Harpers Ferry

Images: NPS gallery.

View of Storer College Campus—Before it was a college, the area it was on, called Camp Hill, served as an encampment for Union and Confederate troops. Listen as you pass underneath on the Appalachian Trail as you may hear the haunting bang of soldiers' drums. Or perhaps hear ghostly students who still go about their daily tasks!

Trip In: 1.1 miles Along Appalachian Trail to Jefferson Rock, past Harpers Cemetery and St Peter's Catholic Church, and to the original site of John Brown's Fort.

At the parking area, cautiously cross the street and follow the dirt path to the *left* as if going back to William L Wilson Freeway. Follow the Appalachian National Scenic Trail to the right as it ascends toward Harpers Ferry and beneath Storer College, a historically significant college for black students opened after the Civil War to teach reading/writing to formerly enslaved people. It became a four-year college for African Americans.

At 0.7 miles, hikers will come across Jefferson Rock, a large stone outcrop, where ghostly soldiers have passed by tourists along the trail and have been mistaken for Civil War reenactors from town—until they vanish from sight!

Jefferson Rock—

For those who find ghostly solace in cemeteries, just above is a side trail to Harper Cemetery, the burial site of early settlers who resided in Harpers Ferry.

Harper Cemetery

Next along the trail is St. Peter's Catholic Church, a powerful icon above Harpers Ferry since 1833. Father Michael Costello was the priest at St. Peter's from 1857 to 1867 and ministered to many during the Civil War. Look carefully before descending into the town of Harpers Ferry by the stone steps as his spirit is occasionally seen around the outskirts of the church, walking as if in deep thought.

Follow the path down the stone steps past Public Way to High Street and turn right, then left on Shenandoah Street to a small hillside and follow the path to the site of Old John Browns Fort.

Original site of John Brown's Fort. The fort, left, and armory buildings.
Image: NPS Gallery.

The fort location now.

On this little hillock was the site of the original "John Brown Fort," which was the Federal Armory's fire engine house and where John Brown and his men, on a daring militant venture against slavery, were captured. Beyond, center, is the fort and its placement now.

Most who visit Harpers Ferry have heard the story of John Brown's anti-slavery raid on October 16, 1859, where he led 21 men, including two of his sons, to seize the U.S. Arsenal located there and where the Shenandoah and the Potomac Rivers meet. His goal was to use the guns to create a vast army of formerly enslaved people, incite a rebellion to free all enslaved people, and after that, create a completely separate state in the Shenandoah Valley for all blacks. He did not succeed and was hanged in Charles Town not long after. His ghost strolls along the streets where the fort once stood.

This is a great place to pause on the hike, grab a bite to eat, and enjoy the many shops in Lower Town Harpers Ferry. Then, after a walk to The Point and for the true tourist adventure, take the C&O Canal Footbridge across the Potomac River before returning to The Point at the Rivers where the second half of the hike begins.

Trip Out: 1.0 miles Short hike along Shenandoah Street to Virginius Island or Hamilton Street Trail back to the Parking Lot:

Looking down at Harpers Ferry from Maryland Heights across the river.

From The Point, follow Shenandoah Street, paralleling the river and past the National Park's historical structures until you get to the bus parking area where Bridge Street intersects with Shenandoah Street. You will turn left here onto Bridge Street and if darkness is falling, beware of the Phantom Runner of Shenandoah Street—

In 1798, this riverfront street bustled with workers and shops and a permanent federal armory producing muskets, rifles, and later pistols for the United States. On a chilly January 29, 1830, 26-year-old Thomas Dunn, the Superintendent of the U.S. Armory at Harpers Ferry, had just returned from his lunch. He entered his office and stirred the fire before sitting near his desk and picking up a book. Dunn was not popular with the workers. He had recently taken the position, hired to improve production rates and quality control, and he was good at his job.

The building to the right of the John Brown Fort was the former Armory superintendent's office. Circa: 1885. Courtesy: Historic Photo Collection, Harpers Ferry NHP.

As the new superintendent, Dunn replaced many incompetent veteran armory workers and refused to hire lazy ones. He did not allow loitering, gambling, and drinking, which the men, up until this point, did quite often instead of working.

To be rid of their new boss, several men banded together with the idea they would murder Dunn. They drew lots with broom corn to see who would be the one to kill Dunn face to face, and 21-year-old Ebenezer Cox, known locally as a young miscreant who liked to drink and gamble, drew the shortest grassy length of broom corn stalk and lost the bet. Cox was desperate and had several times asked Dunn for a job, but the man turned him down. He had been hovering around the armory for quite some time, still enraged.

Cox slung a musket over his shoulder and walked blatantly down the street and into Dunn's office. He asked the man for work, and Dunn denied him.

Cox raised his gun and shot Superintendent Dunn in the chest, killing him. Cox rushed from the building and out onto Shenandoah Street, where law enforcement discovered him hiding in a waterwheel house. The courts hanged Cox for his crime, but his ghost still visits Harpers Ferry. He runs along Shenandoah Street, always looking over his shoulder while he makes his way to the waterwheel house.

Shenandoah Street during earlier days.

Shenandoah Street nowadays.

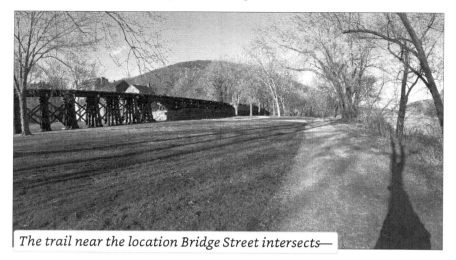

The trail near the location Bridge Street intersects—

Bridge Street connects with Virginius Island Trail and Hamilton Street (both will lead you along the river) and back to the parking lot through the abandoned ruins of a cotton mill, the Shenandoah Pulp Factory, and where many other buildings once stood. Keep a watchful eye out for spirits of the town's past. Travelers along this trail have witnessed bobbing lantern lights and shadows of people from days long gone!

An old cotton mill along the trail—

Haunted Hikes of the Appalachian Hills & Hollers 2

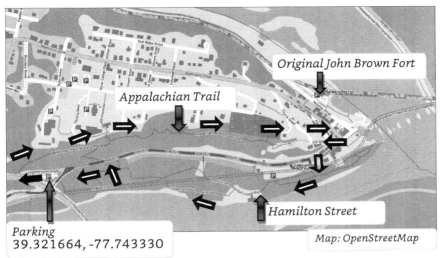

Parking
39.321664, -77.743330

Map: OpenStreetMap

Parking: (Do not forget to pay for this parking!)
River Access Parking Lot | Public Parking
Shenandoah Street
Harpers Ferry, West Virginia 25425
(39.321664, -77.743330)

At the parking area, make a left as if you are going back to William L Wilson Freeway (watch for traffic turning off the highway). Hikers will note a dirt path that parallels the highway for a short distance, then turn into the Appalachian National Scenic Trail. Follow this dirt path into Harpers Ferry, then return to the parking lot via the Virginius Island Trail along the river.

Hike to Harpers Ferry: About 1.0 miles. Dirt trail. Moderately strenuous with uphill climbs and rugged rock steps.
Beginning at the Parking Lot to downtown Harpers Ferry via the Appalachian Trail—

Hike back to Parking: About 1.0 miles. Easy. Dirt path and asphalt road running along the river.
Return to the Parking Lot from The Point and Shenandoah Street, then along Hamilton Street/Virginius Island Trail.

Ohio

Lonesome Lock

Lonesome Lock in 1910—Image: NP gallery—

Between 1825 and 1832, Irish and German immigrants dug by hand a 328-mile inland water route through Ohio's wilderness to connect Lake Erie in Cleveland to the Ohio River at Portsmouth, named the Ohio & Erie Canal. Boats were pulled along the waterway by a team of horses or mules walked by handlers, called drivers, along a path.

At certain points where the water was less navigable, typically because the land was not level, watertight chambers with entrance and exit doors were added to fill with water from a nearby stream while a boat rested within. The boat would raise or lower (depending upon which direction it was heading) with the water, and then a worker on the far side opened the exit door so the boat could enter back into the canal. These devices were called locks. Along the canal were the thriving towns of Peninsula and Boston. Between the two, via the canal path and in a remote section, was Lock 31, also known as Lonesome Lock.

A driver and mules pulling a boat along the Ohio & Erie Canal—

More than just canal boat drivers walked the course because the towpath provided a straight footpath from town to town for residents as well. Unfortunately, in the more isolated areas like Lock 31, where the surrounding area was swampy much of the year, it was also a place for thieves to secret themselves and prey on those who passed by stealing money, mules, and horses.

Sometime during the canal's operation, a man taking the towpath was ambushed and beheaded by robbers at Lock 31. Afterward, his ghost would roam the lock area searching for his head. Many a canal boatman refused to go through the lock after dark and would tie up at docks at Peninsula or Boston for the night, then go through the next morning.

Lonesome Lock nowadays with towpath trail, rear—

Now over 80 miles of the Ohio & Erie Canalway has been restored into a trail by Cuyahoga Valley National Park. A section passes by Lock 31, Lonesome Lock. And if you hike the trail, you might see the headless ghost that the boat captains saw many years ago!

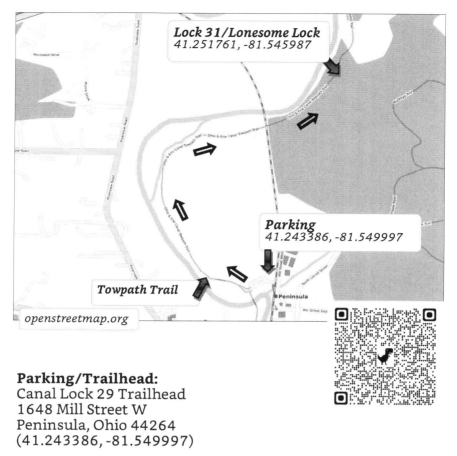

Parking/Trailhead:
Canal Lock 29 Trailhead
1648 Mill Street W
Peninsula, Ohio 44264
(41.243386, -81.549997)

Hike: 1.0 miles, one-way. Out and back. Level towpath trail. The graveled/dirt path leads to Lock 31 (41.251761, -81.545987) and other historical features along the way with interpretive signs. Hikers can continue along a boardwalk to Stumpy Basin and farther for longer hikes.

Vinton County Parks—Moonville Tunnel
Vinton County, Ohio

The Moonville Brakeman

Moonville Rail Trail and tunnel—

In the early days of the railroad, trains were slowed or stopped by turning a wheel on top of a railcar. The men who turned these wheels were called brakemen; their job was incredibly dangerous. They had to climb up a ladder to get to the top of the railcar to reach the wheel, and they also had to jump from railcar to railcar because it usually took more than one brake to slow the train.

The brakemen worked in all seasons regardless of the weather. Many slid on the slippery surface of the railcar roof and tumbled to their death in rainy and snowy weather. Others died when they failed to duck as the train barreled into a tunnel. The brakeman's job was stressful, and some of these men turned to drinking. One such brakeman was going along the track from Zaleski and almost to Moonville one night. He held a bottle of whiskey in his hand, which he sipped along the way. The more he walked, the more he sipped. The more he sipped, the drunker he got. The drunker he got, the more tired he began to feel until, at some point, he decided to take a nap. All would be fine with taking his little drunk slumber except for three things: he used the rails as a pillow, the track as a bed, and sometime during the night, a train came along and took off his head. His head bounced in one direction, over the track and down into a small ravine where Raccoon Creek was flowing heavily. His body flopped to the other side of the path and lay neatly tucked into the brush. The bottle spun around for ten seconds in the center of the tracks and then came to a stop without sloshing out much whiskey at all.

The next morning just before dawn, a miner heading from Moonville to the Zaleski mines in drizzling rain came across the bottle of whiskey lying on the tracks. "What a find!" he exclaimed and reached down to pick up his prize. Just as his fingers touched the glass, he heard a raspy voice call out, "That's mine!" The miner's head shot up. He looked left to right but could not find the source of the voice. Then his eyes dropped to the bed of the tracks, and he saw little specks of blood and followed them up and over the rail and to the area where the train track ballast stones stopped. He reached out, parted the thick brush, and there before him was the corpse of the brakeman. But there was no head.

The miner ran to town just as it began to storm and formed a party to return and bury the body and search for the brakeman's head. However, nobody ever found the head along the train tracks to Moonville or in the deep recesses of Raccoon Creek that was overflowing its banks because of the heavy thunderstorms.

For several days, townspeople searched, but the location of the head was a mystery. Most believed it was washed far downstream, never to be found. The whiskey bottle was largely forgotten. It lay there for years in the center of the tracks because anyone who reached down to pick it up never let it stay in their grasp for long as they were nearly scared to death when the ghost of the brakeman called out quite clearly, "That's mine!"

A ghost hike and hunt at Moonville in the dark. Moonville Tunnel is one of the places I have offered haunted night hikes with storytelling and ghost hunting. Each time I take folks to the sites, we get some kind of mysterious paranormal activity.

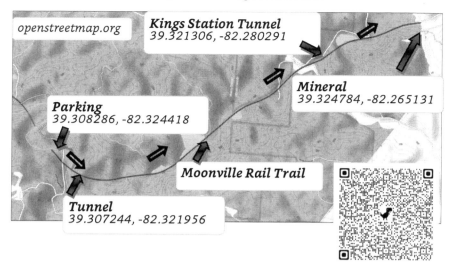

Parking: Designated parking near Moonville Tunnel.
Hope-Moonville Road
McArthur, Ohio 45651
(39.308286, -82.324418)

Hike to Moonville Tunnel: Hike 0.2 miles, one-way. Out and back. Along a maintained rail-trail path (Moonville Rail-trail). Mostly flat.
Tunnel: (39.307244, -82.321956)

Longer Hike—Moonville Tunnel to King Tunnel: 2.7 miles, one-way. Out and back. One way. Easy hike along a level gravel rail trail. The trail will pass the old ghost town of Ingham Station (no buildings) and then to Kings Station Tunnel.

Longer Hike—Moonville Tunnel to King Tunnel to Mineral: Moonville Tunnel/King Tunnel/Mineral: 3.5 miles, one-way. Out and back. Easy hike along a level gravel rail trail. The trail will pass the old ghost town of Ingham Station (no buildings), Kings Station (one building remaining), the wooden King Tunnel, and then to Mineral.

Bring bug spray as marsh/wetlands surround the area. You may also need a flashlight as the tunnels are dark, and the riding stables that use the path do not remove manure from the trail.

Ohio State Parks & Watercraft
At Lake Hope State Park
Peninsula Trail
Vinton County, Ohio

The Night Watchman

Peering through the woods from the Peninsula Trail at the old Hope Furnace, center, looking for a bobbing light on top signaling a spirit.

In the mid-1800s, there was a furnace processing iron ore where Lake Hope State Park now stands. Hundreds of men worked there, timbering the hills for the wood burned to make charcoal to fuel the furnaces, working at the furnace, or hauling the ore.

Hope Furnace in the 1800s.

Little remains but the ruins of the furnace chimney. It is enough, though, to harbor a ghost. Sometime during the years that the furnace made the iron, a night watchman overlooking the structure fell to his death into the fiery pit. Almost immediately after, when the bosses would have their meetings in one building on the property, there would be several loud bangs upon the door. When answered, nobody was there.

Hope Furnace today—

It was not easy keeping workers during the night watch, too, as a phantom lantern would follow the path of the dead man's last walk through the building and disappear as it came to the pit. Even now, hikers taking the Peninsula Trail that, at a certain point, passes nearby the furnace have seen a curious bobbing light hovering in mid-air where the building once stood around the chimney.

Entrance to the Peninsula Trail. I have learned from experience to always mark my starting location on my cell phone mapping app before I leave for a hike in case the trail is not well-maintained or poorly marked. This trail is a prime example of this safety tip as it is not clearly indicated with blazes or common identifiers, and many little spurs lead to park cabins, fishing spots, and where the trail had been bypassed due to fallen trees, mud holes, and sections collapsing off the hillside. It is a good habit to get into, marking spots along the route, as not all private and public properties appoint a specific and trained staff to maintain their trails.

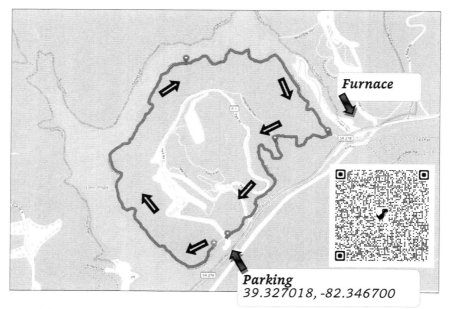

Parking/Trailhead:
State Route 278/Lodge Road
McArthur, Ohio 45651 (39.327018, -82.346700)
There is a gravel pull-off along State Route 278 just before the entrance to Lodge Road. It is a loop trail. Hikers will see one sign noting the trailhead (start or finish) on the same side of the road as the parking area. A secondary trailhead (start or end) is also on Lodge Road's opposite side, just past the park signage. Either can be chosen for the loop.

Hike the Peninsula Trail: 2.8 miles. Loop. The trail follows the park lake proper on a fairly level, tree-lined path with some short ups and downs, then turns along a finger of the lake before passing Hope Furnace (a side trail can be taken to see the furnace up close here: (39.3324920, -82.3423918). To do so, hikers will need to walk along the roadway. After, the trail ascends slowly before working back down to the parking area. The course has no blazes or markers but features a couple of map signs along the route. Seasonally mucky and slumpy in areas.

Hope Iron Furnace
Lake Hope State Park
OH-278
McArthur, Ohio 45651
(39.331976, -82.340552)

After Dark

The lower trail at Conkle's Hollow in the Hocking Hills has a legend—

Just a little off Big Pine Road near the South Bloomingville region of the Hocking Hills and in an area that has never been more than sparsely habited, there is a deep, dark hollow. Few people have ever lived there long because of strange happenings. Those walking nearby on certain nights hear deep moans and screams issue from the bowels of the valley. Three men were murdered here, and it is their voices carried with the wind. The story of their downfall and the spirits that possess this deep pocket of earth is passed on as this—

During the mid-1700s, flatboats carried families along the Ohio River and the many smaller streams, searching for a safe place to settle with fertile farming lands. There were many fights between the settlers and Shawnee and Delaware over the territory, and attacks on travelers were common. One such group of warriors set out to rob flatboats as they came through a narrow, shallow pass along the Ohio River. Once they raided the passengers, they would flee into the unsettled areas of the wilderness, pausing long enough to conceal their stash in the many small caves of southern Ohio. One of those areas is now known as the Hocking Hills region.

After several such raids, word traveled about the dangerous and shallow pass where Shawnee ambushed boats. Some voyagers tried to avoid the pass along the river altogether. Others had no choice but to pray heartily, row quickly through with the possessions they carried, and take the chance Shawnee or Delaware would waylay their boats. One expedition was especially fearful of taking the route. They had brought with them all they owned, and among their possessions was a chest filled with many precious silver coins.

The frightened settlers developed a plan to elude the Shawnee at this point on their journey. They sent one flatboat ahead with the women, children, and their goods. Just behind would be a posse of men, horses, and guns in a second boat lying in wait and ready to stop the thieves. Yet, on this particular trip, a band of three Shawnee hijacked the boat. As the warriors seized upon their treasures and opened the chest filled with coins, they delighted in their good luck, but they failed to question why there were no men among the boat passengers until it was too late. Then, the second flatboat with the men and weapons rounded the bend in the river and came upon the thieves.

Horsehead Grotto at the Conkle's Hollow lower trail. It gets its name from the horsehead-shaped stone at its entrance.

The posse landed their boat, jumped to their horses, and grabbed their guns to give chase. They pursued the three warriors relentlessly for days. At some point, the three Shawnee, believing they had outrun the posse, slowed as they came into a dark valley between two high hills with a small stream running between them. They rested there a day, stuffing their loot into the nooks and crannies of the sandstone cliff walls, handfuls of coins thrust within and back to the end of the narrow creek valley where they could go no farther as it ended in a sheer cliff wall. There they stopped and readied to leave. But not before the thieves heard the sound of horses huffing in the cool, damp air.

One Shawnee looked back and, realizing they had trapped themselves within the hollow, prepared to fight, but the settlers outnumbered them. There was no escape, and the posse murdered the men within the recess.

The settlers found some stolen goods, but no one ever recovered the many silver coins. Their whereabouts were a mystery. Not long after the murders, the place almost immediately became a terrifying area to visit after dark. Moans and groans swept out from the hollow, and ghosts played pranks on those walking within as if they wanted to keep them out.

Along the trail and between high cliffs. Hikers must remain on the trail, be out by dusk, and no pets are allowed in the preserve.

According to one of the volunteers who helps with the state park activities, strange things do occur within the hollow after dusk. Things bang and bump and groaning is heard when the wind whips up and works its way through the belly of the hollow. Once, when she was setting up Tiki bamboo torches along the trail with several young volunteers so visitors could see the path during a night hike at Conkle's Hollow, something peculiar happened with her group on that new moon night which was very dark.

The crew had yet to light the torches, waiting until it was completely dark outside. The four dawdled at a small cave in the bend of the trail and readied with rechargeable lighters and matches to fire up the dry torch wicks—

"When we felt it was dark enough, we all picked a torch to light but as hard as we tried, we could not get any of them to light," she divulged. "Every time we lit a match, it was like a puff of someone's breath blowing it out. Every time we flicked the lighter, it simply would not give us a flame. We had to stagger blindly all the way back to the parking lot in the pitch-black for more matches. All the while, it was deathly quiet except for a low, hushed whisper we prayed was the creek. Not even the sound of crickets or a deer bumbling around in the leaves in the dark came to our ears. We returned, and suddenly, the old lighters seemed to work, and the crickets and birds started chirping again." The night hike went on as planned. However, that same little group of help never volunteered to walk back through Conkle's Hollow after dark again!

Conkle's Hollow Upper Rim Trail—

Parking/Trailhead:
Conkle's Hollow State Nature Preserve
24132 Big Pine Road
Rockbridge, Ohio 43149
(39.453491, -82.573374)

There are 2 Trails to hike, Upper Trail and Lower (Gorge) Trail:

1) Hike Lower Gorge Trail: 0.6 miles, one-way. Out and back. Wheelchair-accessible trail.

2) Hike Upper Rim Trail is a looped trail that is 2.0 miles long. This hike may be considered strenuous for those who are not physically fit, do not hike regularly, or have health issues such as knee surgeries or heart problems. It involves a moderate to steep incline, uneven steps, 70 to 100-foot cliff drops, paths with visible roots, and steep terrain. It is not suitable for young children.

Wayne National Forest
Tinker's Cave
Hocking County, Ohio

Ghostly Horses and the Dead Horse Thief

Tinker's Cave (also known as Dead Horse Thief's Cave) is haunted by a thief named Shep Tinker, who was always up to some shenanigans. On one occasion, Tinker was riding through the country on a Sunday, and as he passed a church, he was mistaken for the circuit riding preacher arriving that morning. He was given a warm welcome and brought into the church. He preached a sermon and was on his way not long afterward without anyone knowing the better!

A man and horses haunt a rock shelter off a lonely stretch of dirt-gravel road at the head of a valley. He died many years ago, and the reason for this haunting might have something to do with the dead man's deeds in life.

It was late one afternoon in the mid-1800s when a lone farmer herded his goats into the backyard of the Buntz House hostel in Logan. The farmer told the inn owner that he had come to town to sell a herd of his goats. He needed a place to stay for the night, but he could not afford the full night's stay up front. He assured the hostel owner that he would pay half now and the rest in the morning and after he sold the goats. As an act of goodwill, he also suggested that the owner could lock the gates with the goats inside his yard as insurance he would not leave without paying.

The farmer was charming and convincing, so the owner agreed to the arrangement, received half the payment, and locked the goats inside the yard. The next morning, however, the goats and farmer had vanished without paying what was due. Only several wooden planks lying askew in the backyard showed how the thief had made his escape—he had placed boards up and over the wooden fence so the goats could clamber over in the dark of night, and he could steal away without unlocking the gates. The farmer was not a farmer but a well-known thief named Shep Tinker, who had stolen someone's goats and needed a place to hide for the night while he fled.

Old newspapers often recall Shep Tinker swindling business owners and terrorizing farmers by stealing their animals all over nearby counties where his well-to-do family had their farm. He hid the livestock in the region's many caves until he could move them to northern Ohio to sell there.

It was rumored Shepherd Tinker helped Confederate soldiers led by John Morgan during their raids through Ohio by giving his men horses stolen from the town of Logan. He spent time in prison off and on. Once, he even charmed a girl, whose job was to bring food to the prisoners, into helping him escape by stealing the warden's keys.

Another time, he stole a black horse belonging to Doctor James Dew. Upon seeing Shep Tinker sneak off with his horse, Doctor Dew took off after Tinker. As darkness came, Doctor Dew had nearly caught up with Tinker, but realizing he was about to be overtaken, Tinker bound the horse's muzzle with a white cloth and turned the horse around until he was heading toward Doctor Dew. In the darkness, Doctor Dew called out to Tinker and asked if the man had seen a rider with a black horse. Tinker said, "Yes, I did! He went thataway!" He pointed Doctor Dew in the direction he had come. The doctor took off again after his horse, not realizing until later he had been tricked by the horse thief!

Shepherd Tinker disappeared after the Civil War. Locals always said that Shep stole horses from the wrong farmer and ended up on the short end of a noose right in the cave where he hid most of his stolen animals and the large rock shelter that bears his name, Tinker's Cave. It also holds Tinker's ghost and the ghosts of the horses the thief filched from their owners. Hikers have heard muffled whinnies and shuffles of hooves inside the cave and the mumbles of Shep boasting about the thousands of horses he stole.

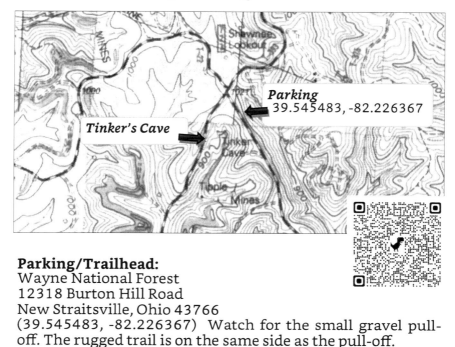

Parking/Trailhead:
Wayne National Forest
12318 Burton Hill Road
New Straitsville, Ohio 43766
(39.545483, -82.226367) Watch for the small gravel pull-off. The rugged trail is on the same side as the pull-off.

Hike: 0.2 miles, one way. Out and back. The path is steep and rugged to the cave (39.544650, -82.227180).

Ohio State Parks and Watercraft: Salt Fork State Park— Stone House Museum Trail
Guernsey County, Ohio

Looking for Bigfoot

*Looking out over **Stone House Museum** and to the expanse of Salt Fork State Park. The forest seems to go on forever and it is not hard to imagine THINGS beyond our imagination are out there—*

People have been crossing paths with hairy bipedal creatures for centuries. Mostly described as human-like, over seven feet, hairy, and foul-smelling, they were once widely known as *Wild Men* or *Hairy Men*. Then logger Gerald Crew found and presented a plaster cast to The Humboldt Times of a huge ape-like footprint from Bluff Creek Valley in California, where he was employed. The newspaper printed his story—"16-Foot Footprint Has Natives in Dither." The title would have *Bigfoot* beneath it. The name would stick.

When conversations arise over the big hairy creature's prime territory in the tri-state area of Ohio, Pennsylvania, and West Virginia, those who know the beast always bring up Salt Fork State Park. Located in eastern Ohio, the park has a whopping 17,229 acres for Bigfoot to inhabit. It has all the makings of the perfect Bigfoot habitat—prey like deer, squirrels, rabbits, and plenty of water on Salt Fork Lake. It has room to roam and plenty of places to remain hidden. Between the mid-1980s and 2018, countless sightings have been at the park. In my many hikes here, I have even heard ape-like calls within that wild area and beyond Stone House Museum, which I cannot explain. No matter how fast my feet run along the trails to catch up to them, they always seem just out of reach. Man or beast or coyote or—? I do not know.

I am not alone. In August of 2004, an ordinary picnic took a horrifying turn when a couple went for a stroll with their dog in the woods. It was a quiet evening, around 7:00 p.m. Then, abruptly, the two began to hear loud howls. The sound seemed to be working its way parallel to their hiking feet. After stopping to take a closer look, the man saw a nearly eight-foot-tall, dark-colored form looking at him and his wife. When reporters at the Daily Jeffersonian in Cambridge interviewed him, the man stated, "What we saw—it was standing there. It was dark - I will not say it was covered with hair —but it was a dark figure standing nearly eight feet tall. I could see its head [move from side to side] like it is looking at me. And then it turns and keeps on walking [down the hill]." Both frightened, the couple retreated to the picnic area, grabbed their belongings, and left.

In another encounter, a couple was camping in the primitive campsites at Bigfoot Ridge. They heard occasional screams as they started to fall deep into sleep in their tent.

*The primitive campsites at **Bigfoot Ridge** where a couple fled the park after a Bigfoot encounter.*

Then, around 1:00 a.m., the sound of something tearing grass from the earth awakened the woman. She waited until the noise faded away. When it quieted, she opened the door to the tent and crawled out, shining her flashlight on the surrounding area. At the edge of the woods, she saw two large, yellowish eyes the size of golf balls staring at her. Then, just as quickly as they were there, they vanished. The couple promptly packed up their site and left, abandoning their tent.

Bigfoot reports come in from one end of the park to the other. At Hosak's Cave, a huge bare footprint was found in 2017. Hikers along the trails have heard whoops, howls, and tree knocks at all times of the year. And occasionally, an image of a huge hairy creature shows up in photographs. Believe it or not, it is always fun to visit and find out for yourself.

*Along the **Stone House Trail** where some have heard the call of Bigfoot. Whoops and hollers have been heard here.*

Map: Salt Fork State Park

Parking: Stone House Trail Parking Lot
Park Road 4
Kimbolton, Ohio 43749 (40.131827, -81.485904)
Trailhead: (40.131300, -81.486418) Across R-4 road.

Hike: 1.8 miles. Loop. Trail passes through a forest and Salt Fork Lake to Stone House (40.127865, -81.499763).

Hosak's Cave—A Bigfoot print was found here.

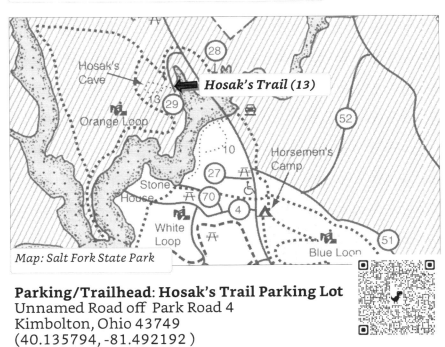

Map: Salt Fork State Park

Parking/Trailhead: Hosak's Trail Parking Lot
Unnamed Road off Park Road 4
Kimbolton, Ohio 43749
(40.135794, -81.492192)

Hike: 0.5 miles. Out and back. Rugged.
(Recess cave: 40.136937, -81.494081). Area closes at dark.

Morgan's Knob Loop Trail—A mix of habitats and along an old road where homes once stood. Their remnants, and perhaps a few ghosts, may remain—along with Bigfoot, as both tree knocks and sightings have occurred here.

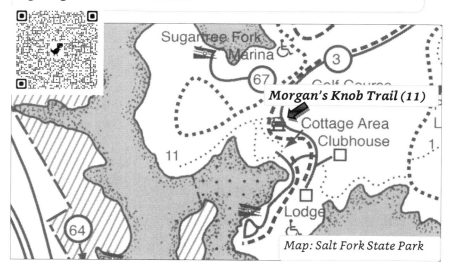

Map: Salt Fork State Park

Parking/Trailhead: Morgan's Knob Trail Parking Lot
Park Road 3
Kimbolton, Ohio 43749 (40.116230, -81.526137)

Hike: 1.4 miles. Loop Trail with an added trip to Morgan's Knob for a short but uphill climb. Old roadbed to dirt path beneath the forest canopy. Watch for the ruins of old homes along the route.

Pennsylvania

Abandoned Pennsylvania Turnpike— Southern Alleghenies Conservancy Pike 2 Bike Trail Sideling Hill Tunnel
Fulton County, Pennsylvania

Those Things That Lurk Within

The creepy and (kind of) abandoned Sideling Hill Tunnel—

There is an abandoned 13-mile section of turnpike in Pennsylvania. The wild is starting to take over. Tall shoots of grass and saplings have fought their way from the darkness below and grappled their way upwards between cracks and fissures of the buckled, gray-black pavement to bask in the sunlight. Brush and tall trees once kept far from its path by an army of road crews have crept up to the solid white edge line like an advancing enemy easing forward, preparing to recapture the land it lost years earlier. Colorful chalk graffiti appears in greens, pinks, reds, and blues.

The old turnpike is on many people's bucket lists to visit, although few have the guts to take this forsaken post-apocalyptic-looking road and follow it through an abandoned tunnel that is 1.3 miles long, pitch-black in some places, and just plain creepy. However, it is not enough that it appears isolated and friendless. There are things of the supernatural, too, that lurk here.

This bit of road was part of the Pennsylvania Turnpike that got its roots from the vision of a mainline railroad in the late 1800s with nine tunnels running across Alleghenies and connecting Harrisburg to Pittsburgh. Workers began constructing the railway and its tunnels using an inactive charter of the South Pennsylvania Railroad, but owners only saw about forty percent of it finished. Then, one of the backers sold his shares to a competing railroad company, and work was stopped cold.

Working on the railway at Ray's Hill Tunnel, about 3.8 miles from Sideling Hill Tunnel. Workers did die during the construction of the Sideling Tunnel in haste to complete it, mostly from explosions and rock falls. Image: Pennsylvania State Archives /Library of Congress

Nearly a half-century later and during the Great Depression, the Motor Truck Association proposed building a toll highway across Pennsylvania on the abandoned railroad bed. This dream became a reality, and the turnpike, dubbed "America's First Superhighway," was created along with toll booths and plazas where drivers and passengers could purchase gas and other items. Workers even enlarged the railroad tunnels to fit two cars.

Along the turnpike in 1942—Image: Library of Congress

One problem from the start was the congestion caused by the bottlenecking of multilane and opposing traffic, having to adjust from two lanes to one when driving through these east-west tunnels. On summer weekends, traffic could be backed up for three hours on the roads. But that was not the only problem. With only one lane of travel and increased traffic over the years, there were many head-on collisions. To resolve these issues and modernize the turnpike in the 1960s, the Turnpike Commission removed three tunnels (Sideling Hill, Rays Hill, and Laurel Mountain) and bypassed the roads. In addition, the Commission eliminated the Cove Valley Service Plaza near the Sideling Hill Tunnel and abandoned that section of the highway.

Haunted Hikes of the Appalachian Hills & Hollers 2

That nobody drives there anymore does not stop people from visiting. And they can come with caution. Southern Alleghenies Conservancy purchased the abandoned turnpike and converted it into a bike trail. You can hike or bike the deserted turnpike and traverse the tunnel for those who dare. Partway, you will even pass the pad for the old plaza, although the building is gone.

Above, hikers and bikers will pass the ruins of the old turnpike plaza along what is now the Pike 2 Bike Trail.
Image: Library of Congress

Right, a plaza before this section was abandoned. It is not difficult to image the ghostly figures of its past showing up once in a while.
Image: Library of Congress

Within the Sideling Hill Tunnel—I am not typically afraid of little children. Still, partway through, seeing a shadow, and recalling that a ghostly girl prowls within, my imagination went swiftly to the dark and terrifying. I got the heebie-jeebies. Thereafter, I frantically biked the tunnel with legs pumping like a bat out of hell, my hair standing on end, and I could not get out of there fast enough.

It is dark and 6782 feet long. When I biked the turnpike, turned around, and returned the way I had come, my light was tiny, and my cell phone lit up a small part of the passageway, so my ride most of the route was completely dark. Ug. It was not bad on the way through. But I had time along that mile to think about all the dark things that creep around inside. Apparently, a little girl died in a car wreck, and her ghost lurks within the confines of the tunnel. Some who have tossed pebbles inside have them launched back at them! And some have seen mysterious car lights from vehicle wrecks from the past.

But what would later grab my attention was that many people have witnessed a Wendigo-type creature that uses it as its lair—this notorious supernatural being of Cherokee history is over 6 feet tall, gray, thin, and hunched over.

Needless to say, they have a certain desire to kill humans and devour their flesh.

The turnpike trail. Due to the loneliness and remoteness of the path, I would suggest exploring this area with others—Bring a flashlight! By the way, the long and narrow Sideling Hill was originally called Side Long Hill because of its length. Early settlers and travelers had to decide whether to take the treacherous, narrow, and steep climbs/descents of the mountain or take the very long way around it. Oh, and on some "hikes," you may note that I use my bike for part or all of a bikeable route. Sometimes, I will journey a good 12-hour drive from one hike to the next. If it is getting dark, I will use my bike to cover the full extent of the trail quickly and to get pictures before dark. Well, and sometimes, I just feel like cycling.

I did not know all these details when I toured the road and tunnel. But it was probably a good thing. Something big enough to cast a shadow shifted and moved with me while I was partway through my return trip. My fist-size bike light only lit a teeny-weeny path before me, and I could not see much out of the range of its circle of dim light a foot before my front tire. I thought the shadowy figure was maybe a deer or my imagination. Still, it was one terrifying, heart-thumping, leg-pumping bike ride before I got back to the other side. I stopped and looked back, trying to catch my breath. I saw nothing but darkness within.

Pike 2 Bike Trail Through Sideling Tunnel—
2.4 miles, one way

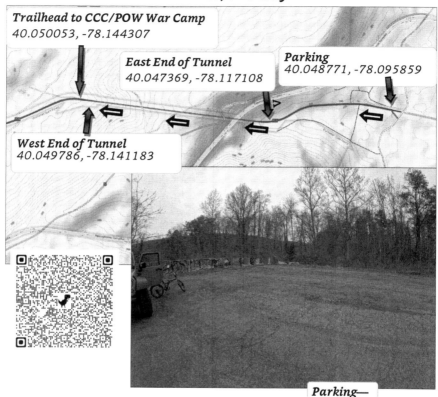

Parking—

Parking/Trailhead:
Pike 2 Bike Lot—
3300-3346 Pump Station Road
Waterfall, Pennsylvania 16689
(40.048771, -78.095859) A short unnamed "dead-end" road with a mailbox at the entrance will lead you directly to the Pike 2 Bike Trail. A section of the old turnpike is barricaded to create the lot.

Hike to Sideling Tunnel: 2.4 miles, one-way. Out and back. Easy on buckled asphalt. The trail slightly descends 1.1 miles along the old turnpike to the tunnel. After, Sideling Hill Tunnel is 1.3 miles long and completely dark at certain points, so bring a flashlight or light source. Watch for broken glass or other debris on the trail/road.

Pike 2 Bike Trail to Sideling Hill Tunnel, Ray's Hill Tunnel, and Ending at Breezewood—
8.5 miles, one-way

Hike to Breezewood (for those who like a longer hike/bike): 8.5 miles, one-way. Out and back. Easy on irregularly buckled asphalt. Trail slightly descends 1.1 miles along the old turnpike to the tunnel. Sideling Hill Tunnel is 1.3 miles long and completely dark at certain points so bring a flashlight or light source. Watch for broken glass or other debris on the trail.

A second tunnel, Ray's Hill Tunnel (40.020689, -78.198326) is 0.6 miles long and located 3.9 miles after exiting Sideling Hill Tunnel (6.3 miles from the parking area). There are subtle rolling hills along the route through this second tunnel that eventually ends another 1.6 miles after exiting Ray's Hill Tunnel and a Pike 2 Bike parking area along U.S. Route 30/Lincoln Highway (39.999973, -78.228077).

Civilian Conservation Corps—Sideling Hill World War II German Prisoner of War Camp
Fulton County, Pennsylvania

Ghostly Remnants of its Past

Just off the Pike 2 Bike trail—ruins of an old Civilian Conservation Corps and German prisoner of war camp that is haunted—

In the 1930s, the Civilian Conservation Corps (CCC) was a federal program that offered jobs to young men to battle high unemployment during the Great Depression. The work was in forestland and designed to open these natural areas for public recreation by building bridges, trails, and roads.

Civilian Conservation Corps workers in Pennsylvania working to clear forest—Image: U.S. National Archives

The government set up one of these sites on Sideling Hill along Oregon Road in Buchanan State Forest called S-52 or Wells Valley Camp. It operated from 1933 until 1937 while the men erected buildings and roadways in the forest. Then, from 1939 to 1940, it was used by Pennsylvania Turnpike construction workers.

In 1941, churches negotiated with the government to set up Civilian Public Service (CPS) camps for young men unwilling to fight in World War II due to religious reasons, also known as conscientious objectors. Instead, they would provide an alternative public service. The churches set up one of the sites at this CCC area where the men offered services like fighting forest fires and erosion control.

From 1945 to 1946, the government used the site as a German prisoner of war (POW) Camp. The men provided labor, paying for their keep by cutting pulpwood timber, mainly used to make paper, with crosscut saws.

Trail and Trail Sign
40.047369, -78.117108

The trail will take hikers to the old officer's residence (right side of the image), and across the street is a kiosk with a map and information about the site and the ruins. There is parking if you wish to drive to the CCC/POW camp. It is located on a gravel road:
Civilian Conservation Corps Sideling Hill (POW) Camp
Oregon Road
Waterfall, Pennsylvania 16689
(40.050662, -78.149137)
Accessing the hiking trail to Sideling Hill Tunnel Hike 2 Bike Trail is to the left of the only building remaining intact, right on the image.

It is just a short, easy 0.25 mile hike off the Pike 2 Bike Pennsylvania Turnpike Trail, not far from the exit of the Sideling Hill Tunnel. Hikers can explore the ruins of the old camp and perhaps see a ghost. Some who visit have been startled by shadowy remnants of its past—dead CCC workers and a ghostly man shouting in German.

Gettysburg, Pennsylvania

U.S. National Park Service
Gettysburg National Military Park—
Spangler's Spring
Adams County, Pennsylvania

The Pale Blue Mist

Spangler's Spring at the south base of Culp's Hill as it appeared during wartime. Retrieved: Gettysburg; the Pictures and the Story—

On the first day of the Civil War Battle of Gettysburg, July 1, 1863, Union troops occupied a meadow on the Spangler family property, a popular picnic area for locals. The site was called Culp's Hill, and both armies highly coveted this position due to its water source—Spangler's bubbling spring flowing into Rock Creek. The Union armies' numbers were strengthened the next day by more troops.

The road/walkway through the battlefield heading to Spangler's Spring.

However, by the evening of July 2, many soldiers were sent to fight at Little Roundtop, leaving about 1400 men to protect Culp's Hill when many Confederate troops attacked. Although outnumbered, the Union was able to hold them back on the upper part of Culp's Hill. However, the Confederates overtook the area near Spangler's Spring where it was located at the foot of the hill. On July 3, the next morning, a huge battle waged until seven hours of heavy fighting later, the Union Army pushed back the Confederates and regained the area around Spangler's Spring.

Legends have always filtered down from one generation to the next that while the battle raged on the evening of July 2, not all enemies fought who came to partake of the fresh, cold water Spangler's Spring offered. At times, it was shared by Union and Confederate alike as if a temporary truce had been called at that spot while battling beneath Culp's Hill.

In the July 1912 Evening News from Wilkes-Barre, a Lieutenant Johnson of Virginia related to reporters that he, himself, had been one of those soldiers who laid down his gun to the enemy there. In the darkness of night, he had captured a New York Volunteer and took his weapon but released his prisoner unmolested. The men prepared to fight again as the sun rose the next morning.

But it is the ghostly figure seen here drawing attention to phantom fare. Some see a pale mist rise near the spring. Then, it forms into a mysterious lady wearing white. Most believe a woman from 1880 committed suicide there after being jilted by her love and she returns mourning her death.

Spangler's Spring nowadays—

Gettysburg Auto Tour Stop 14, Major General Slocum's monument, and not far into Slocum Avenue from Wainwright—
(39.819449, -77.224646)

Here and as if right beside us, my daughter and I clearly heard drums tap-tap-tapping as if a drummer was readying for a battle march. Then, we heard a loud explosion like the firing of a cannonball!

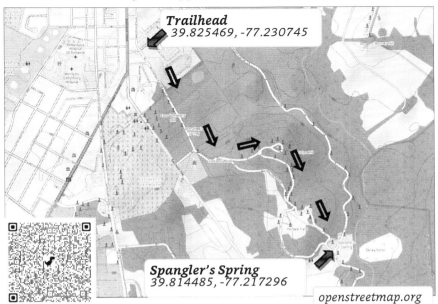

Parking/Trailhead: There is street parking in Gettysburg downtown (or book a room at a number of hotels/bed and breakfast inns like Sleepy Hollow, where I stayed in town, making it incredibly easy to access all the areas).

Hike: Unity Park to Spangler's Spring
Unity/Alumni Park
37 Lefever Street
Gettysburg, Pennsylvania 17325
(39.825469, -77.230745)

Spangler's Spring
Geary Avenue/Colgrove Avenue
Gettysburg, Pennsylvania 17325
(39.814485, -77.217296)
1.3 miles, one way. Out and back, mostly flat. Hikers take Wainwright Avenue and straight onto Slocum Avenue until it ends at Geary and Colgrove avenues. These roads are part of the Gettysburg Auto Tours, so cars make their way slowly along the streets as they pass through the battlefield. The area is closed at dusk/dark. The road is wheelchair accessible, although there are hills.

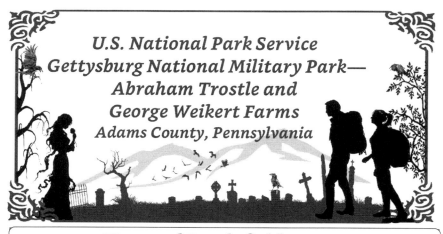

Haunted Battlefield Farms

The Abraham Trostle Farm—

At the time of the Civil War, Abraham and Catherine Trostle lived on a farm, along with their children. However, when the roar of cannons and gunfire grew too close, they fled their house to a safer location. It was a good decision. On July 2nd, 1863, when fighting was heavy, Captain John Bigelow was ordered to hold his 9th Massachusetts Battery position at the farm no matter the cost. Confederates had broken through the Union lines on the Emmitsburg Road, and the Union needed to hold off advancing Confederates.

The 9th Massachusetts' desperate last stand was futile; Confederates overran the Union soldiers and forced a retreat to Cemetery Ridge. In the struggle, the attacking Confederates deliberately shot Union artillery horses so the men could not maneuver the cannons. They lost at least sixteen battery horses and countless soldiers, yet they still managed to buy time for the Union Army. The farm would become a field hospital for the dying and wounded, and horse carcasses littered the yard.

The reek of over 116 dead horses enveloped the area for days. Living on a farm myself, I have taken in rescue horses older than the hills that spend their dying days happily feasting on specially hand-cut alfalfa, moistened beet pulp, and high-end feed. But when they finally pass on, their ghastly stench hovers in the air dead-deer-on-a-hot-August-highway-style. The lingering stink seeps through doors and closed windows and dawdles there uninvited. So it is no surprise to me that even now, visitors to the old Trostle Farm have caught the ghostly stench of death and dying and the rotting corpses of those poor, long-gone horses.

Along the trail—

The George Weikert House—

Not far along the road, there is another haunting that has less to do with scent than it does with sound. The George Weikert House was one of several homes belonging to the immediate family of George Weikert (three of his sons) and a distant cousin. It was a field hospital during the fighting, and surgeons piled amputated arms and legs high outside the home's doors. At least six soldiers died within the walls, and when the family returned, graves filled the yard. The long-dead have returned. Former tenants have divulged they heard heavy, pacing footsteps treading over and over in the attic. Doors open and shut on their own—one so much that a worker nailed it closed.

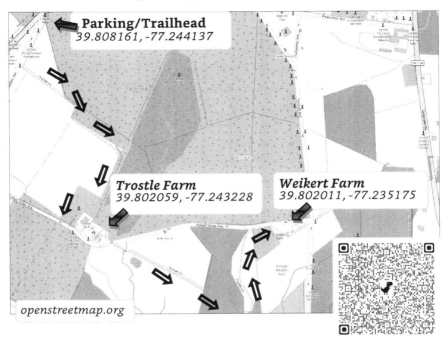

Parking/Trailhead:
Emmitsburg Road, Gettysburg, Pennsylvania 17325 (39.808161, -77.244137) Small gravel pull-off.

Hike: 1.3 miles, one-way. Out and back. Relatively flat. Easy. The trail follows a dirt road to the Trostle Farm and the Weikert Farm.

There is a small pull-off along Emmitsburg Road near the 11th Massachusetts Volunteer Infantry Regiment Monument. Here, hikers will begin along a dirt road and dirt paths through fields.

The trail intersects with United States Avenue at the location of the **Abraham Trostle Farm**: (39.802059, -77.243228)

After crossing the street, hikers will continue on the dirt road and will see that it again parallels United States Avenue before turning at the **George Weikert Farm**: (39.802011, -77.235175)

Left Behind: Little Round Top & Devil's Den

The battle of Gettysburg—view from the summit of Little Round top.

About 2 miles from Gettysburg and one of two rock-strewn hills, Little Round Top and a boulder-ridden area below called Devil's Den were a part of the Civil War battlefield, fought over on July 2, 1863.

Devil's Den

There is a place that, on the surface, looks like nothing more than an inhospitable section of abandoned land with scattered boulders, raggedy trees, and a marshy stream called Plum Run, with sparsely enough water to call a creek.

Standing atop Little Round Top and looking down at Devil's Den—

However, what appears like a wasteland today has a history of great importance—and it has ghosts. Because on the second day of the Battle of Gettysburg, July 2nd, 1863, fighting at this rock outcrop, fittingly dubbed Devil's Den, was intense, bloody, and violent. Almost 8,000 men would battle as General Lee's Confederate troops attacked Major Sickle's Corps of the Army of the Potomac.

It was a victorious battle for the South amidst many defeats on their side that day as the Union troops retreated. But, it was a loss for the many men who would die in that battle, brought down one by one as a result of Confederate sharpshooters who moved into the safety of the rocks and clefts of Devil's Den, firing nearly effortlessly and picking off Union soldiers and officers atop Little Round Top.

They come back, those dead. Visitors come home with ghostly images of a mysterious headless rider on horseback. They also see ghostly apparitions quite often, and camera batteries die around the site, returning to normal after tourists have gotten into their cars and pulled away.

Johlene Riley, a local author, gives a possible explanation for this occurrence in one of her books, *Ghost Encounters of Gettysburg*. She says that war photographers would come in after the battles and stage the soldiers' bodies and weapons, moving them to different locations to make them more dramatic or suitable for a story. Perhaps this discourtesy to the corpse was not appreciated by the dead. They return the disrespect by eking out the energy within camera batteries—and the reason some folks have found blurry images of long-dead soldiers.

Along the trail at Devil's Den where a dead soldier's photograph was taken right after the battle—

Mark Nesbitt, a historian and writer on Gettysburg and its ghosts, worked as a park ranger at the National Military Park. He chronicled hundreds of stories of the paranormal in the area—one he relates is of a young woman climbing the huge boulders dotting the landscape at Devil's Den.

She felt something snatch at her ankle. Shocked, she looked down into the dark crevice beneath her. Staring back at her was a man wearing a Civil War uniform. When she screamed, he vanished!

On my last hike through the area of Devil's Den, the huge rock formation where a bloody battle played out, a woman was pacing back and forth frantically, trying to catch her breath. I assumed she had just hiked the hill to the top of the boulders and back, but I asked her politely if she was alright. She told me "yes" and "no," throwing her hands out between us to display them trembling furiously because she had gotten quite a fright. Upon taking the trail from the top of Devil's Den downward, she lingered to catch her breath near the base of the huge boulders and peer within the crevices. Someone was standing inside, and she smiled courteously, thinking it was one of the parents watching their children climbing on the rocks. It appeared to be a man, his silhouette murky and almost blending into the shadows of the recess. He keeled slightly forward and seemed to lean hard against the stone before completely vanishing!

Devil's Den's most well-known ghost story is that of the barefoot Texan soldier with long tousled hair and outfitted in a flimsy government-issue butternut shirt. He is quite unkempt and donning a floppy slouch hat with a dented crown and the front flipped up. When he walks up to visitors, he points at Plum Run and greets hikers with: *What you're looking for is over there.* Then he disappears.

Some men of the 1st Texas—Image: The Photographic History of The Civil War in Ten Volumes, 1911

But why would the spirit of a Texan soldier show up there? The 1st Texas Infantry Regiment got their nickname the "Ragged Old First" from their scruffy clothing and bold battle stance. When they first left Texas, they were so poorly armed and uniformed that many brought their guns from home, and some did not have any weapons at all.

During the fight at Devil's Den, the 1st Texas Infantry Regiment, although incredibly outnumbered, fearlessly pushed forward and drove the Union's artillery guns and the soldiers out of the boulder-ridden chunk of land.

Then, quickly, 1st Texas sent in sharpshooters who began to take out Yankee officers on Little Roundtop. There were 1,800 Rebel casualties during this fight, and one of them, in his butternut shirt and floppy slouch hat, has returned to greet visitors at the park.

Little Roundtop

Standing atop Devil's Den and looking up at Little Round Top—

On the morning of July 2nd and in the heat of the Battle of Gettysburg, only a few Union soldiers stood atop a barren but boulder-ridden hilltop south of Gettysburg, the extreme left flank of Union lines. The larger forces were laid out just a bit to the north. However, this little piece of higher ground, almost overlooked by Union commanders, would, within the next July-sweltering twenty-four hours, become a significant turning point for the war. Just a handful of Union soldiers fought against repeated assaults from much larger troops of Confederate soldiers to hold them off.

If the Confederates had seized Little Round Top that day, they might have invaded the entire Union Army's left flank and perhaps won the battle. Instead, Union soldiers feverishly rushed to the location and immediately opened fire. The intense and bloody fighting at Little Round Top began with Confederates charging the hill and their sharpshooters, protected by the rocks at Devil's Den just beyond, returning fire. Finally, the 20th Maine Regiment, nearly out of ammunition after holding off the enemy for almost an hour and a half, made a daring charge down the hill to defend Little Round Top. On that day, 134 of the 2,996 Union soldiers died from their wounds. More than 279 of the 4,864 Confederates lay dead. Many of these struggles were by bayonet point as the Union soldiers began to run out of ammunition.

Little Round Top and trail—

Visitors have reported hearing gunshots, cries of battle, and the beat of a soldier's drums here. During the filming of the Civil War movie *Gettysburg* in 1993, several extras on the set were taking a short break on Little Round Top.

After hearing a rustling of leaves, they glanced over to see an old Union soldier in a tattered private's uniform. He reeked of the sulfur odor from the black powder used in old muskets. A stubbled beard covered his chin and wrinkled cheeks. He made it quite clear he was angry that a battle was taking place. "Rough day, boys?" he grumbled at them. He then held out his hand and gave the actors some spare rounds of ammunition before he left along the trail, disappearing. The strange encounter unsettled the group enough that they had the musket rounds checked. Sure enough, they were genuine, not the fake prop ammo used for the set!

If you love Gettysburg and its ghosts, I have a whole lot of stories just like these in my book, "Little Book of Gettysburg Ghosts."

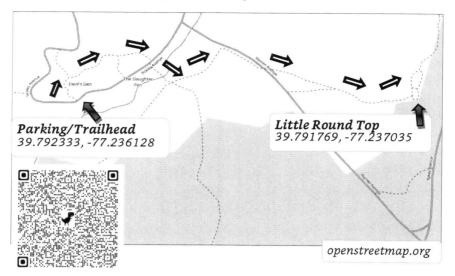

Parking/Trailhead:
Gettysburg National Military Park
Devil's Den Parking
Sykes Avenue
Gettysburg, Pennsylvania 17325
Parking/Trailhead: (39.792333, -77.236128)

To Little Round Top: (39.791769, -77.237035)

Hike: 0.4 miles, one-way. Out and back. Hikers follow the trail above Devil's Den, then up to Little Round Top—a mix of dirt paths and walkways with natural stone mixed with concrete. I would recommend going out of season, as tourists throng to the area at certain times, like the anniversary of the battle and summertime. Pull up a mapping system before visiting and check out the many trails around these sites. There are so many trails off the beaten path with the possibility of ghosts to explore! You may need to improvise—the battlefield sites are sometimes upgraded and closed. For example, on one visit, Little Round Top was inaccessible. I hiked a trail directly across from Devil's Den that began near the parking lot and after the bridge over Plum Run (39.791386, -77.241146). It was a nice, quiet hike through the woods and to Round Top. I was disappointed at first, not being able to visit Little Round Top, until along the way, I felt two ghostly tugs on my shirt and hushed, cautionary voices! It was as if someone did not know the battles were over, and he was warning me to stay away.

Monterey Pass Battlefield Park & Museum
Old Maria Furnace Road
Franklin County, Pennsylvania

Hellhounds on his Heels

This path, as I am told, is haunted. Along this road, Maria Furnace Road, while heading toward Monterey Pass, Confederate cavalry tried to fight off an attempt to block the road. After the battle, 2/3 of the Confederate army marched along this very route. Years later, a man traveled these old roads to evade the law after a murder—

On February 1, 1893, eighteen-year-old Emanuel Monn seemed to vanish off the face of the earth about ten miles from Gettysburg. It appeared very suspicious to those who knew him well in the tight-knit community where almost everyone was closely related, if not by blood, by marriage.

At the time, he was sharing a small cabin with 34-year-old Henry Heist on the George Reese property near Maria Furnace, just a few hundred feet from the Reese home. The two were cutting out a meager living together as local woodchoppers, working for a farmer named Henry Herring.

Nothing appeared amiss until someone brought up the point of a small incident occurring on the night he disappeared. Emanuel and Henry had been invited guests at a small gathering at the Ann and George Reese home on Wednesday, February 1. Henry Heist had left early. There had been an argument between Henry and Emanuel. Henry had threatened the Reese daughter, Susanna McCleaf, who was also his step-niece, for flirting playfully with Emanuel. Family members had noticed Susanna and Emanuel sweetly holding hands in the cozy kitchen that evening, teasing each other and awkwardly dancing as young folks do. The two had even talked excitedly to Susanna's mother about Emanuel escorting Susanna to visit family on the far side of the mountain near Old Forge in the upcoming week. Henry overheard the conversation. Witnesses noted at the Reese home that it angered Henry so greatly that he slapped Susanna hard enough to send her across the room.

Not long after Henry left the Reese home, Emanuel Monn had headed out with a quick goodbye and said he was returning to the cabin. He seemed cheerful; he was playing his mouth harp happily. That was the last any of his friends and family would see of the young Emanuel alive. Henry showed up in Emanuel's place to take Susanna to see her family, stating the young man who shared his cabin had left town. During the outing, the two visited Emanuel's family, living in the vicinity, who questioned the story that Emanuel had left without telling anyone.

Emanuel's father began to enquire where his young son had gone, as did the nearby families at Maria Furnace.

Authorities questioned Henry; he denied knowing anything. It is not surprising. Henry was not new at this game and knew how to play it—he had already spent time in jail. In 1887, he was found guilty of shooting another man, assault, and battery and sentenced to three years in prison. In 1891, he received a sentence for robbery. He would never confess or offer clues to incriminate himself. However, he would sell the cabin and all inside, including an ax and blanket belonging to Emanuel Monn. He came up with a few feeble stories and excuses for the teen's disappearance—one even included blaming George Reese, stating Emanuel and George had fought, and Henry had discovered the body with George hovering over it. Henry had even gone as far as describing George Reese trying to cut off Emanuel's head because it would not fit in the scanty hole dug in the frozen ground.

On March 12, a search party combing the hillside of Reese's property discovered Emanuel's body 2,185 feet from the cabin in a shallow grave, a pile of brush, flat rocks, and logs overtop. A little digging exposed the toe of a boot sticking out, and then Emanuel lying on his back. Someone had crushed his skull with a hatchet or hammer and made a cut to his throat 3 ½ inches long, which appeared to have been made with a hatchet, while pulling Emanuel's head back. A significant wound lay at the back of the left ear, looking as if made by a succession of blows going deep into the brain. The murderer had severed Emanuel's windpipe and nearly cut off his chin. Henry's victim, young Emanuel, was buried in the old Forge Cemetery in Franklin County.

Henry took off down the road with a posse hot on his heels, complete with baying hounds—through Tomstown and Mont Alto. Authorities nearly caught Henry in Graefenburg. However, he was able to elude the law for almost two months, running the backroads and hiding with family. Finally, he turned himself in to police in Gettysburg.

They hanged Henry at Gettysburg on January 17, 1894. Henry Heist's conviction was based entirely on circumstantial evidence—his jealousy of Emanuel's relationship with Susanna. Nobody came forward to claim his body after hanging. The county buried the corpse in the potter's cemetery at the county home. Throughout the region, rumors prevailed that thieves had robbed Heist's grave, and the body had vanished. However, on Sunday, January 20, the steward of the almshouse, ex-sheriff Elias Fissel, and his son George opened the grave and casket and found nothing disturbed. A marble slab was placed on his grave with Heist's name, date of death, and the word "HUNG." The word "HUNG" was chiseled from the stone, but by whom it is not known

Henry Heist's grave is at the Alms Cemetery in Gettysburg. You can see at the bottom where someone took great care of chiseling "Hung" out. Old Alms House Cemetery—Howard Avenue, Gettysburg, Pennsylvania 17325 (39.844800, -77.227150)

Henry Heist was the last man hanged in Adams County, in Gettysburg. He may be dead, but his ghost lives on. In the old days, folks avoided Maria Furnace Road after dark and any dim and gloomy path south and west of Maria Furnace.

For it was rumored Heist's wicked spirit lurked in these deep and dark cubby holes on cold winter nights, forever evading the men who hunted him down. The ghostly hounds are at his heels, still hell-bent on finding him, bounding after him and baying long and hard into the night. But these particular hounds are not planning on bringing his earthly form for judgment. They chase his soul so that eternal justice is served, and he is dragged straight down to hell.

The Maria Furnace Road—It is well-marked and easy to follow with historical signage of the Battle of Monterey Pass— Hours are 8:00 a.m. to dusk but may change, and hikers must stay on the trails.

A battle ensues with a wagon train during the Civil War as it did along the Maria Furnace Road—

But avoiding Heist's ghost along the trail is not the only spirit hikers may encounter. Some say ghostly soldiers linger here. Immediately after the Battle of Gettysburg, as the Confederate Army began their retreat with a long line of wagons, battle-weary troops fought along this mountain ridge in a thunderstorm on July 4 and 5, 1863 in what is called the *Fight of Monterey Pass*. The Union was able to capture prisoners and destroy hundreds of the wagons.

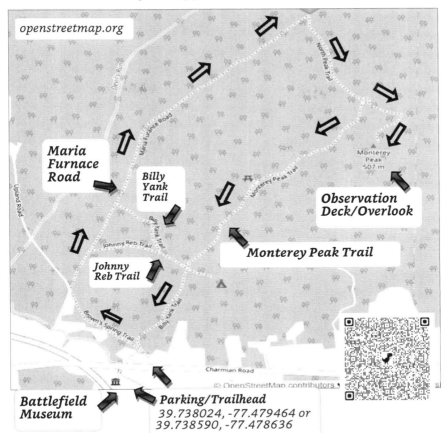

Parking/Trailheads:
1)Monterey Pass Battlefield Park and Museum (There is a short path to the trails from the museum and parking area.)
14325 Buchanan Trail E
Waynesboro, Pennsylvania 17268
(39.738024, -77.479464)
         or
2)Monterey Pass Trail Parking
Charmian Road
Waynesboro, Pennsylvania 17268
(39.738590, -77.478636)

Trail: 1.9 miles. Loop. There are also short intersecting trails (Johnny Reb/Billy Yank). The path has interpretive signs showing battle areas/interesting information. There is a side trail to Monterey Peak with a beautiful overlook. Hikers begin the route at the parking area and follow Brown's Spring Trail to the left to Maria Furnace Road. Follow the old road to North Peak Trail and the observation deck. Return via the Monterey Peak Trail to the parking lot.

Citations

North Carolina—
Brown Mountain:
—Warren, Joshua P. (n.d.). Brown Mountain Lights Morganton, NC A Viewing Guide. Great Guide Offered by Discoverburkecounty.com - Contact agency for details.
—How to find Wiseman's view of the Linville Gorge wilderness. (2022, May 27). Retrieved from https://www.nctripping.com/wisemans-view-linville-gorge-wilderness/
—Linville Falls Lodge & Cottages 8890 NC-183, Linville Falls, NC 28647. (n.d.). A 2-minute walk from Linville Falls, this rustic seasonal lodge off Highway 221 and just a short drive to Wiseman's Overlook.
—Spraker, H. (1922). The Boone family: A genealogical history of the descendants of George & Mary Boone who came to America in 1717 - The Linville Family, Pge 538. Tuttle Company- Rutland, VT
—Story of John Williams contributed by Dianne Fletcher via The Architectural History of Yadkin County, North Carolina , by Yadkin Co. Historical Society, Pgs. 150 & 152 Surry County, North Carolina Wills 1771-1827: Annotated Genealogical Abstracts ,by Jo White Linn, Pgs. 144 & 145. (n.d.). Retrieved from https://www.ancestry.com/sharing/19901205?h=5bd6b1

Grandfather Mountain:
-History of grandfather Mtn. (2022, October 20). Retrieved from https://grandfather.com/history/
-Maya Jarrell. (2022, October). In the mountains: Ghost stories and folktales in the North Carolina high country. Retrieved from https://www.lmc.edu/about/news-center/articles/2022/ghost-stories-itm.htm#:~:text=The%20Phantom%20Hiker%20of%20Grandfather%20Mountain&text=The%20ghost%20of%20a%20lost,by%20tourists%20over%20the%20years
-Carmichael, S. (2020). *Mysterious tales of western North Carolina.* Arcadia Publishing.
-Forrest Gump curve. (2022, June 22). Retrieved from https://grandfather.com/forrest-gump-curve/
-Ghost of grandfather mountain. (2016, May 11). Retrieved from https://www.wsoctv.com/living/features/ghost-grandfather-mountain/819159913/
-Phantom hiker of grandfather mountain: From North Carolina folklore at Americanfolklore.net. phantom_hiker_of_grandfather_m.html
-Retrieved from cherokeelanguage.org/details/30824/Black+eagle

Roan Mountain/Cloudland Hotel:
-Retrieved from https://www.johnsoncitypress.com/living/features/a-stay-and-three-meals-at-the-cloudland-hotel-2-50-please/article_ff7b13c3-2880-51a5-ae46-fa1d00c67784.html

-Retrieved from History of Roan Mountain. http://www.roanmountain.com/area-information/history/
Gay Miller @ Book Units Teacher. (n.d.). Colonial America [Daniel Boone]. Retrieved from https://bookunitsteacher.com/colonial_america/daniel_boone.htm
-The ghostly choir of roan mountain. (2018, May 12). Retrieved from https://mountainlore.net/2018/05/12/the-ghostly-choir-of-roan-mountain/

Roan Mountain/Rhododendron Gardens:
-Whitener, Rogers. "Ghost herd of Roan Mountain." Folks Say and Folks Do. *Kingsport Times-News.* Sunday March 30, 1975

Chimney Rock:
-The chimney rock apparitions. (n.d.). Retrieved from https://northcarolinaghosts.com/mountains/chimney-rock-apparitions/
Eury, P. (n.d.). 'Little people' guarded hickory nut Gorge path vital to the Cherokee. Retrieved from https://www.smliv.com/stories/little-people-guarded-hickory-nut-gorge-path/
-Full text of "Myths of the Cherokee" - Page 333
-Yitnwi Tsundsdi. (n.d.). Retrieved from https://archive.org/stream/mythsofcherokee00moon/mythsofcherokee00moon_djvu.txt
-Yunwi Tsundsdi', the little people of the cherokees (Tsvdigewi, Tsundige'wi). (n.d.). Retrieved from https://www.native-languages.org/morelegends/yunwi-tsunsdi.htm
-The " little people" of hickory nut Gorge! (2015, May 2). Retrieved from https://hickorynutgorgehikes.wordpress.com/the-little-people-of-hickory-nut-gorge/
-Asheville Citizen-Times (Asheville, North Carolina) · 19 Jun 1939, Mon · Page 33 Dancing Fairies Strange Mirages in Chimney Rock Area Described as Indians as Ghostly Tribe. (n.d.).
-The chimney rock apparitions. (n.d.). Retrieved from https://northcarolinaghosts.com/mountains/chimney-rock-apparitions/
-Kendall, E. A. (1809). *Travels through the northern parts of the United States, in the years 1807 and 1808.*
-Weekly Raleigh Register (Raleigh, North Carolina) · 15 Sep 1806, Mon · Page 4 Extraordinary Phenomenon. (n.d.).

Devil's Courthouse:
-Balsam mountains. (2018, October 26). Retrieved from https://appalachian.org/protect-2/where-we-work/balsam-mountains/
-Design, M. (n.d.). Visit the great smoky mountains and Jackson County North Carolina. Retrieved from https://web.archive.org/web/20070630193837/mountainlovers.com/content_outRef_searchRock.asp
-Full text of "Myths of the Cherokee". (n.d.). Retrieved from https://archive.org/stream/mythsofcherokee00moon/mythsofcherokee00moon_djvu.txt

-Kanuga – Chenocetah's Weblog. (n.d.). Retrieved from https://chenocetah.wordpress.com/tag/kanuga/
-Mooney, J. (1891). *James Mooney's history, myths, & sacred formulas of the Cherokees: containing full texts of Myths of Cherokee.*
-North Carolina. (n.d.). Retrieved from www.sherpaguides.com/north_carolina/mountains/balsam_mountains/middle_prong_wilderness.html#Devil
-The slant-eyed giant. (n.d.). Retrieved from www.firstpeople.us/FP-Html-Legends/TheSlant-eyedGiant-Cherokee.html

Noland Creek Trail:
-Bones Found In Swain May be J.C. Hunter's. (n.d.). Asheville Gazette-News (Asheville, North Carolina) · 10 Nov 1911, Fri · Pg 8.
-Bones in Tree May Solve 12 Year Mystery. (n.d.). The News of Henderson County (Hendersonville, North Carolina) · 24 Jul 1922
-Cemeteries of Swain County, NC Pearlie M. Brendle Compiled by the Historical Records Survey of North Carolina: 1940. (n.d.).
-Much Speculation as to Man's Identity. (n.d.). Asheville Citizen-Times (Asheville, North Carolina) · 3 Nov 1911, Fri · Page 6.
-North Carolina has new Murder Riddle. (n.d.). The Dispatch (Lexington, North Carolina) · 7 Feb 1912, Wed · Page 1.
-Olde Swain. (n.d.). Noland Creek was home (A story of the Cole Hyatt family, part II). Retrieved from https://reflectionsofoldeswain.blogspot.com/2013/09/noland-creek-was-home-story-of-cole.html#:~
-Private Investigations for the Missing. (n.d.). Gone in the smoky mountains: Trenny Gibson's disappearance. Retrieved from https://investigationsforthemissing.org/blog/f/gone-in-the-smoky-mountains-trenny-gibsons-disappearance
-Vanished into thin air at the great smoky mountains. (n.d.). Retrieved from https://mysteriousuniverse.org/2016/08/vanished-into-thin-air-at-the-great-smoky-mountains/

Virginia—

Corbin Cabin:
-Stony Man Trail Hikes to Beautiful Shenandoah Views. https://www.funinfairfaxva.com/stony-man-trail-shenandoah-virginia/
-George Corbin interviewed by Edward Garvey, transcribed by Victoria M. Edwards. (n.d.). Retrieved from commons.lib.jmu.edu/cgi/viewcontent.cgi?article=1023&context=snp
-Potomac Appalachian Trail Club, "Corbin Cabin Work Trip (1953)," Appalachian Trail Histories, accessed March 4, 2022, https://appalachiantrailhistory.org/items/show/93. (n.d.).

Pocosin Mission:
-Far Pocosan, or, Pocosin mission; Shenandoah National Park – Abandoned country. (2013, July 8). Retrieved from https://www.abandonedcountry.com/2013/01/07/far-pocosan-wild-with-moonshine-whiskey/

-Gifford, E. (2021, March 12). Hike to upper Pocosin mission at Shenandoah National Park. Retrieved from https://gohikevirginia.com/pocosin-trail/
-Pocosan: The land of whoops and whippoorwills. (2016, February 25). Retrieved from https://piedmontvirginian.com/pocosan-the-land-of-whoops-and-whippoorwills/

Gap Cave
-Retrieved from https://www.nps.gov/cuga/learn/nature/upload/cave-handout2.pdf
-http://www.nps.gov/archive/cuga/cudjo.htm.

Pound Gap Massacre:
-Ira Mullins. (n.d.). Retrieved from https://www.findagrave.com/memorial/16007729/ira-mullins
-Johnson, C. A. (1938). A narrative history of Wise County, Virginia,.
-Nature hike scheduled on red fox trail, site of the 1892 'Killing rock massacre' - The mountain eagle. (2018, July 19). Retrieved from https://www.themountaineagle.com/articles/nature-hike-scheduled-on-red-fox-trail-site-of-the-1892-killing-rock-massacre/
-Pound gap massacre ~ Killing rock. (2013, September 22). Retrieved from https://www.opencaching.us/viewcache.php?wp=OU06A5
-Tabler, D. (2021, July 13). The killing rock massacre of 1892. Retrieved from https://www.appalachianhistory.net/2017/09/the-killing-rock-massacre-of-1892.html
-Harrisburg Daily Independent Harrisburg, Pennsylvania 27 Oct 1893 Preached his own Sermon
-The red fox of the mountains by John Fox Jr. 1901. (n.d.). Retrieved from https://yeahpot.com/taylor/redfoxhanging.php
-https://www.timelinesmagazine.com/publications/civil-war-courier/the-rebel-trace-the-forgotten-mountain-road/article_672e6a7c-af42-11ea-817d-874313cf5808.html

Kentucky—

Mammoth Cave:
-Mammoth cave National Park (U.S. National Park Service) including a tour guide during a visit. (2022, December 5). Retrieved from nps.gov/maca/index.htm
-Taylor, B. (1860). *At home and abroad: A sketch-book of the life, scenery, and men.*
-Wheeling Sunday register March 04, 1894 The Ghost of Mammoth Cave. (n.d.).
-When tuberculosis patients quarantined inside Kentucky's mammoth cave. (2021, July 14). Retrieved from www.smithsonianmag.com/travel/when-tuberculosis-patients-quarantined-inside-kentuckys-mammoth-cave-180978144/

Sloan Valley Tunnel:
-Get maps. (n.d.). Retrieved from ngmdb.usgs.gov/topoview/viewer/#15/36.9391/-84.5582

-Semi-weekly interior journal. October 24, 1890 Many Killed.
-The Washburn leader. October 25, 1890. (n.d.).
Clear Creek Hollow Trail:
-Hammon, N. O. (1970). EARLY ROADS INTO KENTUCKY. The Register of the Kentucky Historical Society, 68(2), 91–131. http://www.jstor.org/stable/23377254
-teva.contentdm.oclc.org/digital/collection/p15138coll23/id/9101/
-boonetrace1775.com/Early-Roads-Into-Kentucky---Neil-Hammon.pdf
-Battle of middle Creek battlefield, map, directions, historical marker, Civil War, 1862. (2022, May 25). Retrieved from https://www.americanhistorycentral.com/entries/battle-of-middle-creek-1862-battlefield-map/
-Carol Crowe-Carraco. (n.d.). *The Big Sandy - The Kentucky Bicentennial Bookshelf*. Western Kentucky University 1979.
-Future President James A. Garfield's report on the Battle of middle Creek, Kentucky. (2019, January 12). Retrieved from https://ironbrigader.com/2019/01/12/future-president-james-a-garfields-report-on-the-battle-of-middle-creek-kentucky/
-Middle Creek. (n.d.). Retrieved from https://www.battlefields.org/visit/battlefields/middle-creek

Maryland—

Stickpile Tunnel-Green Ridge State Forest:
- Green ridge / West Portal of Stickpile Tunnel/B135.5. Great site for reference with images of the old railroad and the buildings originally created by Jeremy Cooper and preserved in his memor by Ed Kapuscinski & Gerald Altizer. www.wmwestsub.us/stickpiletunnel.htm
-https://dnr.maryland.gov/forests/Documents/greenridge/GRSF-SFMP-2019.pdf. (n.d.).
-Most people have no idea this unique tunnel in Maryland exists. (2016, June 30). Retrieved from https://www.onlyinyourstate.com/maryland/tunnel-in-md/

Great Falls Maryland Mine:
-Gold mine trail – C&O canal trust. (n.d.). Retrieved from https://www.canaltrust.org/pyv/gold-mine-trails/
-Maryland Mine. (n.d.). MARYLAND HISTORICAL TRUST M: 29/27 Magi # INVENTORY FORM FOR STATE HISTORIC SITES SURVEY. Retrieved from https://mht.maryland.gov/secure/medusa/PDF/Montgomery/M;%2029-27.pdf
-McClearly/McCleary/Carey were the initial mine owners. (n.d.). Retrieved from https://pubs.usgs.gov/bul/1286/report.pdf
-Thomson, Lila H Gold Fever Gripped Miners. Montgomery County Sentinel. Volume, June 21, 1962, Page A2, Image 2. (n.d.).
-By JOHN C. REED, JR., and JOHN C. REED. (n.d.). *Gold Veins Near Great Falls, Maryland*. GEOLOGICAL SURVEY BULLETIN 1286: https://pubs.usgs.gov/bul/1286/report.pdf.

Burnside's Bridge:
-Burnside bridge (U.S. National Park Service). (2021, November 7). Retrieved from https://www.nps.gov/places/antietam-battlefield-burnside-bridge.htm
-Ghosts of Antietam's battlefield and the bloody lane - Back in time - General highway history - Highway history - Federal highway administration. (2017, June 27). Retrieved from https://www.fhwa.dot.gov/infrastructure/back1105.cfm

Canal Boat Ghosts—Monocacy/Stickpile/Paw Paw/Haunted House Bend/Lander Boat Ramp
-Conococheague aqueduct - Chesapeake & Ohio canal National Historical Park (U.S. National Park Service). (2020, May 13). Retrieved from https://www.nps.gov/choh/conococheague-aqueduct.htm
-Hahn, Thomas F. (1980). C. and O. Canal Boatmen, 1892-1924. American Canal & Transportation Ctr.
-Hahn, Thomas F. (1991). Towpath Guide to the C & O Canal, Georgetown to Cumberland. American Canal And Transportation Center.
-The Rock Hall Ghost. (n.d.). The Monocacy Monocle. Ghost Stories of the Monocacy: https://monocacymonocle.com/images/issues_2019/MM_2019-10-25.pdf.-The Baltimore Sun Baltimore, Maryland 06 Jun 1999 New Life in the Old C&O Canal. (n.d.).
-https://mht.maryland.gov/secure/medusa/PDF/Allegany/AL-I-C-006.pdf. (n.d.).
-Paw Paw Tunnel C & O Canal National Historical Park Maryland. (n.d.). http://npshistory.com/brochures/choh/paw-paw-tunnel.pdf The C&O Canal's Great Tunnel.
-2 Mile Level 48.96 Waste weir. (n.d.). Chesapeake a Ohio kanál. Retrieved from https://wikijii.com/wiki/chesapeake_and_ohio_canal#Waste_weirs,_spillways,_and_informal_overflows_(mule_drinks)
-https://mht.maryland.gov/secure/Medusa/PDF/Montgomery/M%3B%2016-32.pdf

West Virginia—

Dorsey's Knob:
-O'Dell, Les Report on Red-Headed Man of Dorsey's Knob. (n.d.).
-Tabler, D. (2021, July 21). The red-headed man: A ghost tale of Dorsey's knob. www.appalachianhistory.net/2020/10/the-red-headed-man.html
-Wiley, Samuel T. History of Monongalia County, WV, from its first settlements to the present time. Kingwood, W.Va., Preston publishing company, 1883. www.loc.gov/item/01007899/
-WVU History Dept. "Dorsey's Knob." Clio: Your Guide to History. July 19, 2021. Accessed 12/18/ 2022. theclio.com/entry/45896.
-http://www.us-data.org/wv/preston/bios/cobun-family.txt

Twin Falls State Park Resort, Falls Trail:
Cook, Jim. (n.d.). Twin Falls State Park: Falls Trail - Headless Ghost of Falls Trail. Retrieved from https://www.tiktok.com/@wycojim/video/6977789808194178310. If you get a chance, take a listen to Cook's wonderful storytelling/video of the ghostly tale!

Twin Falls State Park Resort, Hemlock Trail
Cook, Jim. (n.d.). Twin Falls State Park: Falls Trail - Headless Ghost of Falls Trail. Retrieved from https://www.tiktok.com/@wycojim/video/6977789808194178310 If you get a chance, take a listen to Cook's wonderful storytelling/video of the ghostly tale!

Rend Trail-New River Gorge National Park:
-Rend trail (U.S. National Park Service). (2022, April 30). Retrieved from https://www.nps.gov/places/rend-trail.htm

Ohio—

Lonesome Lock:
- Medina Sentinel on May 28, 1925. Captain Doc Seeley article.
-Retrieved from http://npshistory.com/publications/cuva/ohi-lock-31.pdf
-History of the Ohio & Erie Canal (U.S. National Park Service). (2021, November 22). Retrieved from https://www.nps.gov/articles/000/history-of-the-ohio-erie-canal.htm

Pennsylvania—

Sideling Tunnel:
-The abandoned Pennsylvania turnpike - Back in time - General highway history - Highway history - Federal highway administration. (2017, June 27). Retrieved from https://www.fhwa.dot.gov/infrastructure/back1007.cfm
-Emartin. (n.d.). Pike 2 bike information. Retrieved from https://www.co.fulton.pa.us/pike-to-bike.php
-Glessner, R. (2022, November 28). Exploring the abandoned Pennsylvania turnpike. Retrieved from https://pabucketlist.com/exploring-the-abandoned-pennsylvania-turnpike/
-http://elibrary.dcnr.pa.gov/GetDocument?docId=3617501&DocName=FD02%20Sideling%20Hill%20CCC%20Hiking%20History%20Map%202020.pdf. (n.d.). Sideling Hill History Trail Buchanan State Forest.
-WeConservePA. (n.d.). Retrieved from https://weconservepa.org/landtrust/one?conservancy_id=4260

Sideling CCC/POW:
-http://elibrary.dcnr.pa.gov/GetDocument?docId=3617501&DocName=FD02%20Sideling%20Hill%20CCC%20Hiking%20History%20Map%202020.pdf. (n.d.). Sideling Hill History Trail Buchanan State Forest.

Gettysburg—
Spangler's Spring:
-1911) Gettysburg; the Pictures and the Story. Gettysburg, Pa. Tipton & Blocher. [Pdf] Retrieved from the Library of Congress, https://www.loc.gov/item/unk82029629/
-Trostle, Kevin, Times Correspondent. (1988, October 31). Ghosts of the Civil War. The Gettysburg Times [Gettysburg], p. 6B.
-Spangler's spring (U.S. National Park Service). (2022, August 29). Retrieved from https://www.nps.gov/places/spangler-s-spring.htm

Little Round Top:
-Fighting Regiments of War of Rights - 1st Texas "Ragged Old First"-https://www.youtube.com/watch?v=WSPDQ1h0zSU
-https://thoughtcatalog.com/jeremy-london/2019/05/14-creepy-incidents-that-happened-at-the-gettysburg-battlefield/
-https://www.liveabout.com/ghost-encounters-at-gettysburg-2594202
-https://monstermovies.fandom.com/wiki/Gettysburg_Ghosts
Aliens and the Antichrist: Unveiling the End Times Deception By John Milor

Devil's Den:
-Quotes from Mark Nesbitt. (2019, August 27). The Ghosts of Gettysburg's Devil's Den. Retrieved from https://history.howstuffworks.com/american-civil-war/devils-den.htm
-https://www.youtube.com/watch?v=S6ErKxIHibk
-https://www.historynet.com/devils-den-gettysburg
-Mark Nesbitt, owner Ghosts of Gettysburg Candlelight Walking Tours and author of Gettysburg ghost books. If you want a whole lot of ghost stories from the area, suggested readings are in his series: Ghosts of Gettysburg: Spirits, Apparitions and Haunted Places on the Battlefield.
-Staged soldiers: https://civilwartalk.com/threads/the-weaver-photographs-at-gettysburg-nov-1863.83786/

Trostle's Farm:
-July 2, 1863: The Second Day at Gettysburg. (n.d.). Retrieved from https://john-fenzel.mykajabi.com/blog/GettysburgSecondDay
-Then And Now Pictures of the Battlefield. (2019, August 13). Retrieved from https://www.nps.gov/gett/learn/photosmultimedia/then-and-now.htm
-The Trostle farm on the Gettysburg battlefield. (2015, February 7). Retrieved from http://gettysburg.stonesentinels.com/battlefield-farms/trostle-farm/

George Weikert Farm:
-http://gettysburg.stonesentinels.com/battlefield-farms/weikert-farm/

-Newman, R. (2017). *Ghosts of the Civil War: Exploring the Paranormal History of America's Deadliest War*. Woodbury, MN: Llewellyn Worldwide.
-https://civilwarwiki.net/wiki/George_Weickert_Farm_(Gettysburg)

Maria Furnace:
-The Gettysburg Times November 12, 1926 - Page 1
-The Evening Sun Hanover, Pennsylvania October 23, 1990 - Page 47
-Standard-Sentinel Hazleton, Pennsylvania September 04, 1893 - Page 3
-The Gettysburg Times October 24, 1959 - Page 4
-The Gettysburg Times October 17, 1959 - Page 6
-https://www.findagrave.com/memorial/59419381/emanuel-mohn
-https://www.therecordherald.com/article/20130104/news/130109953
-The Shippensburg News September 08, 1893 - Page 2

Made in the USA
Middletown, DE
29 August 2023

37367718R00161